The Pot Thief Who Studied Ptolemy

The Pot Thief Who Studied Ptolemy

A Pot Thief Mystery

J. MICHAEL ORENDUFF

OPEN ROAD
INTEGRATED MEDIA
NEW YORK

Copyright © 2009 by J. Michael Orenduff

Cover design by Kathleen Lynch

ISBN 978-1-4804-5879-6

This edition published in 2014 by Open Road Integrated Media, Inc.
345 Hudson Street
New York, NY 10014
www.openroadmedia.com

To a fine colleague and true gentleman,
Clyde Tombaugh (1906-1997).
Your tour of the heavens continues, my friend.

The Pot Thief
Who Studied
Ptolemy

1

If you're looking for a hero, you've come to the wrong place. I lack the iron will and steel nerves the job requires.

I lead a calm and contemplative life, selling pots by day and digging them up by the light of the moon. I used to excavate in broad daylight. We called it treasure hunting in those days. Then Congress passed the Archaeological Resources Protection Act, turning me into a pot thief and my day job into my night job.

My shop is in Albuquerque's Old Town where I get about as much human contact as I do out in the dunes. The price tags on my merchandise—at least four digits to the left of the decimal—create long dry spells between buyers. Few opportunities to chat with customers, even fewer to process their MasterCards.

Technically, I'm a criminal, but I don't think what I do is wrong. I have scruples. I never dig on reservations or private land. Let the Indians and the landowners do what they please with their patches

3

of earth. I stick to public land. I figure I'm part of the public, so why shouldn't I have the right to prospect on our land?

I love being alone under the bright desert stars with only the spirits of ancient potters for company. I'm a sucker for the lure of buried treasure, the thrill of the hunt, the satisfaction of the find. It's hard to describe the pleasure I feel when I find a long-buried pot, overwhelmed by knowing I'm the first person to touch it in a thousand years. Sometimes I think it might be better than sex.

But how would I know that? I've been living like a monk. It's not easy meeting women when you're on the wrong side of forty-five, only five six and live in the back of your shop.

I'm not abstemious in other matters. I enjoy margaritas at Dos Hermanas Tortilleria most every weekday with Susannah Inchaustigui. Don't worry about pronouncing her family name—it's Basque. Our watering hole is romantic in a rustic way, but it doesn't help my chastity thing. She and I are just friends. But it sure puts an end to my silence. Susannah's quite the talker. Although we discuss anything that comes to mind, the conversation frequently turns to her love life and my illegal adventures, both of which fate seems to delight in contorting.

On this particular evening, the chartreuse emulsion in our glasses had sunk perilously low as I told Susannah about some pots I wanted. They were not on public land. They were stashed in the Rio Grande Lofts. With my constitution, just the thought of skulking around a building full of people sets my stomach churning. Which makes it all the more difficult to understand why I broke in there seven times, got trapped in its basement and seduced in its elevator.

I jiggled the ice around in my glass hoping to generate another sip and said, "The longer I looked at the place, the more it resembled Fort Knox."

"What's Fort Knox look like, Hubie?"

I shrugged. "I have no idea."

"Then how do you know Rio Grande Lofts looks like it?"

"It's just an expression, Suze, like 'solid as the Rock of Gibraltar'."

"I don't suppose you know what that looks like either, do you?"

She knew I didn't because I don't travel. "I've seen pictures of it in insurance ads."

"But you've never seen a picture of Fort Knox?"

"They don't advertise. Can we get back to the point I was trying to make?"

"You had a point?"

I turned up my palms in mock exasperation. "I've forgotten."

"Maybe a second round would jog your memory." She waved to the willowy Angie, who brought us fresh margaritas quicker than you can say Quetzalcoatl. We lounged under the west veranda enjoying the last warm rays of a dry October evening. I dipped a chip in the salsa and washed it down with the first swallow of my new drink. Like Albuquerque in autumn, the salsa and drinks at Dos Hermanas are unfailingly refreshing.

"The point I was trying to make is that getting into the Lofts is going to be difficult. I don't think I can do it."

"I have confidence in you," she said. And then she gave me that enigmatic smile, eyes narrowed, only the left side of her lips bowed. "You've broken in to better places than that."

"I've never broken in to anything," I protested.

"You broke in to that apartment in Los Alamos."

"I didn't break in. You kicked in the door."

"You tried to get in by stuffing some of your potting clay in the bolt hole, remember? But it didn't work."

"That's because I only put the clay in a little ways."

"You know what the Church says about that, Hubert: Penetration, however slight, constitutes the offense."

I smirked. "The Church may have lost a bit of its moral authority on sexual matters."

"Good point." She scrolled an imaginary one in the air. "But there was that house in California."

"Okay, I committed one break-in. But I didn't steal anything. I'm not a burglar."

"So you keep saying. But you steal old pots."

"They don't belong to anyone, so it's not stealing."

Here came that smile again. "What is it? Finders-keepers?"

"Exactly."

"No offense, but if you dug in my grandmother's grave to get her wedding ring, I'd consider that stealing."

"So would I. But I don't rob graves. And the stuff I dig up is a thousand years old. Surely there should be some statute of limitations."

"But that stuff belonged to somebody's ancestors," she persisted.

"We don't know that. For all we know, the ancient peoples of this area died out and the current tribes moved in from elsewhere."

"You don't know that."

"True," I said, warming to my subject, "but here's what I do know. All of us—black, brown, red, yellow, and white—are descended from a woman we anthropologists call the African Eve who lived in the Rift Valley about two-hundred-thousand years ago."

"In the Garden of Eden?"

"I don't know if it was Eden, but it was where humans first appeared on the scene, and every human being alive today is descended from that woman."

She gave me that Mona Lisa smile. "Come on, that's just a myth."

"Maybe she didn't chomp on an apple, but she's no myth. The scientific evidence proves it. There's a genetic marker in our mitochondria."

"I think there's a vaccine for that now."

"Joke if you want to, but genetics proves we're all one family, so I have as much claim to the loot in the ground as anyone else."

"So at the end of the day, you and I are both African Americans?"

"All of us are."

"I'll drink to that."

We clinked our glasses together.

Susannah left for class. She's in her late twenties and brings youthful enthusiasm to my occasional illegal capers. When she's not drinking margaritas or kicking in doors, she waits tables two blocks from my shop at La Placita and attends classes three nights a week. She studies art history but changes majors the way most people change socks. She may be working her way through the University of New Mexico catalog.

I graduated from UNM with a business degree and returned a couple of years later to study anthropology and archaeology. I unearthed some valuable pots during a summer dig. They weren't from the official excavation site. I figured out a better place to dig and hit pay dirt.

Literally. I sold the pots to a wealthy collector for more than I earned during my two years as an accountant. I viewed the money as a reward for having a better sense of where to dig than the professors who supervised the project. Digging up old pots wasn't illegal back then, but the university didn't care about legal quibbles. They expelled me.

"Can I get you another one, Mr. Schuze?" Angie's dark eyes peered at me from under those long lashes. How could I say no?

I sipped a fresh margarita as my mind drifted to those coveted pots. I've been hooked on digging up old pots ever since that fateful summer. It isn't just the money. Every touch of that clay connects me with the ancient potter. I suspect she is proud it lasted so long. I even fancy she's happy I've found it.

I use the pronoun 'she' because anthropologists such as Margaret Ehrenberg have argued convincingly that women invented agriculture and created the first pots to carry the seeds and store the grains. My sense of connection is one potter to another, two fellow humans who walked the same earth and dipped our hands in the same clay.

Because of the reverence I feel for ancient potters, it pains me to sell their works. I make sure the buyer appreciates the piece. The best thing I can do for the ancient potter is find a good home for her work. Of course, if a few thousand dollars find a good home in my pocket, then the pain of parting is sweet sorrow indeed.

Although passage of the Archaeological Resources Protection Act made it illegal to dig up old pots, doing so carries little risk. After all, the places one digs for ancient pots are deserted. The same cannot be said of buildings, especially residential ones.

So I should have been worrying. But the margarita was frosty and the sun warm, and my worries evaporated in the desert air.

2

I recall watching from the windows of my social studies class at Albuquerque High School as the steel framework for Rio Grande Lofts rose skyward. Miss Hinkle's lectures couldn't compete with cranes and girders.

The structure started life as an office building with retail space at the street level. It was the third or fourth tall building in town. In my high school naïveté, I assumed we were headed towards a skyline like Manhattan, which—like the Rock of Gibraltar—I've seen only in pictures. Opened during a recession, the place never achieved full occupancy. Downtown shopping lost its battle with suburban malls. The property changed hands several times and hosted a variety of ventures whose only common denominator was failure. Eventually, rent from the few occupants failed to cover expenses, and the place was boarded up.

Albuquerque's latest revitalization plan encourages people to live downtown, and—surprisingly—it's working. Even my old high

J. MICHAEL ORENDUFF

school has been converted to lofts. The boarded-up office building also got a facelift. The ground floor was converted to a lobby
with an entrance vestibule, mailboxes and storage space. Floors
two through eleven were carved up for residences. I suppose calling them lofts was meant to conjure images of exposed brick, high
ceilings and industrial elevators. I was interested to discover if they
really had that look.

But you already know that curiosity about architecture wasn't
the reason I wanted to break in.

Apartment—excuse me—*loft* 1101 was occupied by Ognan
Gerstner, the recently retired chairman of Anthropology and
Archaeology at the University of New Mexico. He was the person who expelled me from the University. I disliked Gerstner, but
that was true before he expelled me. I hold no grudge about it. So
revenge was not my motive for wanting inside the building.

Gerstner forced out Professor Walter Masoir shortly before
I returned to school to study Anthropology and Archaeology.
Gerstner convinced the department to divest itself of its Native
American artifacts. Masoir was the only holdout to this politically
correct plan, arguing quite reasonably that it makes no more sense
to operate an archaeology department without artifacts than it
would to operate a chemistry department without test tubes.

The artifacts were eventually returned to the tribes. At least most
of them were. One collection of rare pots allegedly never found its
way back to its pueblo. The evidence for this was weak—a statement by a now deceased resident of that pueblo claiming they never
received the pots. And the probative value of that statement was
devalued further by the fact that the person it was told to was none
other than Walter Masoir, hardly a disinterested party.

As I mentioned, Masoir was gone before I started my studies,

10

but I read his work and talked to students who knew him. I came to admire him from afar. Proving the plan he opposed was at least partially a failure would have been satisfying. But you can probably guess that vindicating an admired professor was also not the reason I wanted to break in to Rio Grande Lofts.

Neither curiosity, revenge nor vindication incited my illicit intentions. I wanted those pots.

3

After leaving Dos Hermanas, I decided to get the pots off my mind by doing a little amateur astronomy. I sometimes select a planet and chart its location every night for a month or so when I know it's going to slow down, come to a halt and head back from whence it came.

Astronomers call this 'retrograde motion'. It's an illusion of course. Planets don't actually turn around. But it sure looks odd. Mars, for example, will stay on a predictable course for almost two years. Then—for no apparent reason—it appears to go in the opposite direction. I don't know who first observed this strange behavior, but the Greeks knew about it thousands of years ago. That's why they called them planets, which means 'wanderers' in Greek. Most people couldn't care less, but the planets fascinate me.

Which is why I stopped by Treasure House Books and Gifts the next morning and purchased a book about Ptolemy, the first person to successfully model the motion of the planets. His theory was that the planets were on a sort of invisible sphere that circles around the earth like a curved glass ceiling. As that ceiling revolves, the planets also go around in circles on the sphere, and those circles within circles explain why they sometimes appear to go backwards. And here's the amazing thing about Ptolemy's system—it still works today. You can use it to predict exactly when a planet will start to back up.

Ptolemy's model of the heavens started me thinking of the lyrics of a song:

> Like a circle in a spiral,
> like a wheel within a wheel
> never ending or beginning
> on an ever spinning reel

I couldn't remember the name of the song and made a mental note to ask Susannah about it. Occasionally I stopped reading and drew circles within spheres just to see if I had the hang of it. Occasionally I looked up when someone passed by. None of the passers-by became customers.

About four o'clock I started checking my watch. It seemed to be doing its imitation of Mars—slowing down. It seemed like it might never reach five, so I gave up at a quarter 'til and strolled toward the plaza, my eyes on Dos Hermanas.

Susannah waited at our usual table. "I know how you can get in to Rio Grande Lofts. Pretend to be a pizza delivery guy."

Her enthusiasm for my projects is a nice counterbalance to my natural caution.

"Wouldn't I need a uniform?"

Susannah is two inches taller than me and has that healthy ranch-girl look of someone who gets up early to throw around bales of hay or whatever it is they get up early to do on ranches. Her hair is fine and not too long—just below the shoulders when it's down—but there's a lot of it, and no matter how she ties it up, it's usually unruly.

She's a bit unruly herself. She's also intelligent, funny and frank.

"You never order pizzas do you? The delivery guys don't wear uniforms. They don't even use company delivery cars. Pizza places are too cheap to furnish transportation or uniforms."

"Do they get paid at least?"

"Basically, they work for tips."

"Hmm. So I could buy a pizza, drive up in my own car, walk up to the doorman in my street clothes and say 'Large pepperoni for apartment 8'?"

"I don't think they normally announce the ingredients, but, yeah, you just tell them you've got a pizza for apartment 8."

"Then what?"

She thought about it for a moment while she sipped her drink. "Well, I've never lived in an apartment with a doorman, so I don't know what happens next. I suppose they call apartment 8 and tell them their pizza has arrived."

"But since they didn't actually order one, I'd be sunk."

"Yeah, but at least you'd still have the pizza."

I laughed and took a sip of my margarita. Proper form calls for rotating the glass after each sip so there's salt on the rim each time you partake. A deep glass with a small circumference may hold enough, but you run out of salt before you run out of sips. Dos Hermanas glasses are slightly wider than they are deep.

A thought finally came to me. "It wouldn't have to be pizza."

"Of course not. You could pretend to be a take-out Chinese guy."

"What would I do, make myself up like Warner Oland?"

"Who's Warner Oland?"

"He's the actor who played Charlie Chan."

"Charlie Chan, the fat guy in the late night movies with the 'number one son'?"

"That's the one."

"Hmm. 'Warner Oland' doesn't sound like a Chinese name."

"It's not. He was Swedish."

"He played Charlie Chan and he wasn't Chinese?"

"Why not? He also played Al Jolson's father, and he wasn't Jewish either."

"That's no big deal. A Swede and a Jew might look alike. But a Swede and a Chinaman?"

"I don't think 'Chinaman' is politically correct these days, Suze."

She looked at me and sighed. "Okay, a person of Swedish origins and a person of Chinese origins."

"They had very clever makeup people in Hollywood in those days."

"Why are we talking about this?"

I shrugged. "Because you suggested I could pretend to be a take-out Chinese guy."

"Geez, do you ever order out any kind of food?"

"No."

"I didn't think so. The guys who deliver take-out Chinese aren't Chinese. You could do it," she said with enthusiasm.

"But they could still call the apartment and ask if they ordered Chinese."

She gave me a look of exasperation. "Well, you suggested it."

"No, I said it didn't have to be pizza. You're the one who made it Chinese. I didn't mean it should be another kind of food. I meant it could be another kind of *delivery*."

"Like flowers?"

"Exactly."

"How would that be better than food?"

"Because they couldn't call the apartment and verify whether they ordered them because people don't order flowers for themselves. They get flowers sent to them."

"If they're lucky. I can't remember the last time a man sent me flowers."

"Sorry, Suze."

"I tell you, my love life is nonexistent. Maybe I need to change majors. What field has a lot of guys in it? And don't say math, because there's no way I can pass a math course. And besides, have you seen those guys in the math department? Most of them are—"

"Suze?"

"Yes?"

"Can we discuss your dating strategy after we figure out how to breach security at Rio Grande Lofts?"

"Sure. Can we order another drink first?"

We did, and we sat waiting for it in companionable silence on the veranda. The westerly breeze had the bite of autumn and the smell of damp creosote like it had rained on the west mesa. The sun dipped below the horizon and the sky glowed purple and orange. We get spectacular sunsets out here.

Angie brought drinks and fresh chips and salsa. I sipped my margarita to make sure it was as good as the last one, and it was.

Susannah asked what I was reading, and after I told her about my new book on Ptolemy, she gave me the razzing she usually does.

"Boring, Hubert. What do you have against books with characters in them?"

"This book has characters—Ptolemy is a character."

"Was he married?"

"I have no idea."

"How about friends? Any crises in his life? What did he look like? Did he ever—"

"Okay, okay, I take your point. But his system of explaining why the planets move like they do was really neat with lots of circles around circles, and it reminded me of a song, but I can't remember the title."

I sang the lines I remembered.

"I love that song. It's called *The Windmills of Your Mind*. It was the theme song for a great movie, *The Thomas Crown Affair*."

"Now I remember. I liked that one, too. Steve McQueen played a millionaire who was a thief on the side."

"No wonder you liked it. But it was Pierce Brosnan, not Steve McQueen."

"Then there must have been a remake because the one I saw definitely had Steve McQueen and was probably made before Brosnan was born."

"And before McQueen died," she added. I looked at her and she just smiled.

"In the new one, Brosnan steals a . . ." She hesitated trying to remember. Finally she said, "uh . . . Monet, I think."

"They made the thief a Frenchman in the new version?"

She gave me a quizzical look. "No, he was American."

"But you said he stole 'monay'—the way a Frenchman might pronounce 'money'."

"No, he didn't steal money. He stole a Monet, a painting."

"The water lily guy?"

"Right."

"No wonder you liked it."

"Yeah, and Pierce Brosnan is hot."

"Anyway, Ptolemy's circles—"

"This is really delicious salsa," she interjected with a sly smile on her face.

I took the not-too-subtle hint and changed the subject. "You think we're harming our health by eating salsa and chips almost every day?"

"It's not like we're eating *chicharrones*. In fact, the salsa is probably good for you since it has tomatoes and a green vegetable."

"But aren't you supposed to have more variety in your diet?"

"Actually, I think it's better to eat the same thing every day. Your body gets used to it and makes the necessary adjustments to digest it and use it to make whatever nutrients you need."

"I don't get it."

"Digestion is just chemistry. Say your body needs a certain protein to make fingernails. That protein is in corn, so when you eat chips, the body shoots some chemicals into the stomach along with the chewed up corn and the needed protein is synthesized and put to use. Now that same protein may be in lots of foods. But if your body is getting it from corn chips and suddenly you start eating spinach instead, then even if the protein is in the spinach, you might not have the right chemicals to extract it because it's different from the corn."

"That's an interesting theory. Did you ever major in biology?"

"No, but I was pre-vet at one time, and I actually passed organic chemistry."

"Pre-vet must have lots of guys in it. Why didn't you just stay in that major?"

"I didn't like the idea of cutting up animals in labs."

"But you were raised on a ranch."

"Right, and I castrated calves and killed chickens, but that's part of ranching. We didn't kill cats and dogs so we could cut them up to study."

"But didn't you realize when you chose pre-vet that you'd be—"

"Are you going to give me a hard time about this, Hubert? Because I don't need that. I need someone to send me flowers, not tell me I wasn't thinking clearly when I chose pre-vet as a major."

"Sorry, Suze."

"Sometimes you get so wrapped up in logic you forget about feelings. You're like Spock, you know that?"

"You're right. But at least I don't have those weird ears."

She laughed and took a big swallow of her drink. She orders her margaritas without salt. If she has any other faults, I'm unaware of them.

19

4

I'd met Professor Masoir's wife last spring when she came to my shop looking for something her husband could buy for their anniversary. She was a charming lady and I enjoyed our brief chat.

I met the Professor himself when he came in a few days later. I didn't chat with him as I had with his wife, but the few words he spoke were music to my merchant's ears—he wanted to purchase a twelve-thousand-dollar pot by the famed Maria of San Ildefonso.

His October return prompted my interest in Rio Grande Lofts. He walked into my shop on Friday and asked, "Would you mind closing your store while we talk?"

I sell maybe three pots in a good month, so closing up for an hour doesn't threaten the bottom line. I locked the door and rotated the laminated plastic sign to closed.

"You know who I am?" he asked.

"Yes. You're the gentleman who wrote me a twelve-thousand-dollar check last spring."

He lifted his chin and gave out a hearty laugh. Masoir is probably in his eighties. He wears a trim mustache on a sunken face. He's slightly stooped and his hands show evidence of a mild palsy. He doesn't look like someone who laughs often, but it was obviously heartfelt.

"A good merchant remembers his customers by the size of their purchases," he said.

"The UNM Business School should be proud of me."

He was momentarily confused. "I thought you majored in anthropology."

"I did the second time, but my first time through I studied business."

"What made you decide to go back?"

"At the time, I thought it was because the work I was doing as an accountant was terminally boring. I got into pottery because I thought I needed to exercise my creative side. But now I think it was because my first time through didn't expose me to ideas, at least to important ones."

"And what important ideas did you find in anthropology?"

"Is this a pop quiz?"

He laughed again. "Old habits are hard to break. I hope you'll forgive the impertinence of a broken-down old professor."

"You are old, but you are definitely not broken down."

He nodded. "My wife says you are a young man of good character."

"I'm happy she thinks so, but she met me only once."

"She fancies herself an astute judge of character, claims she has a sixth sense about people."

"Perhaps she does."

"I doubt it. But regardless of how she comes to her judgments about people, she is almost always on the mark."

"So you depend on her for accurate character appraisals?"

"After sixty years of marriage, Mr. Schuze, I depend on her for everything." He hesitated for a moment. "Do you have a place where we can sit down?"

"I'm sorry," I said, feeling like a dolt for keeping a shaky eighty-year-old man on his feet. I took him back to my living quarters and sat him in my reading chair. I turned a kitchen chair to face him and asked if he wanted anything to drink.

"Is it five o'clock?" he asked with a wry smile on his face.

"No sir. It's only a little after two."

"Then water if you don't mind."

He took a sip and kept the glass in his hand. "I see we passed through your studio to get here. I gather you've addressed the creative side you spoke of."

"I'm afraid you gather incorrectly. I call it my workshop, not my studio. I make replicas of pots. I don't think of myself as an artist."

"You're too modest. Most people who call themselves artists these days are decidedly not. Someone dumps a crucifix in a jar of urine and calls it art. At least your copies display craftsmanship."

"I agree they do. I'm not modest about that. Maybe it's because I respect the originals I copy."

He sipped his water and nodded his head as if he shared that respect with me. "You know how they ran me off?"

"The story circulating in the department was you opposed the department's plan to divest itself of its Native American artifacts."

"You state it very diplomatically, but I suspect that wasn't how you heard it."

"I think the official characterization was you 'demonstrated insensitivity to the strong link in tribal culture between people and the products of their hands and the unique cosmology of such peoples that rejects the western linear concept of time and posits a timeless link with their ancestors'."

"You remember that?"

"Not verbatim. But I think it's close."

"Probably. It sounds like the twaddle in use back then. If they had said I failed to appreciate that Indians like their pots better than we like ours, their position would have sounded not only false, but—worse from their perspective—trivial. Academics fear nothing more than being thought trivial."

"Ironic," I commented, "since triviality is the essence of academe."

"No wonder they kicked you out!"

"So do you think Indians value their artifacts more than people of European descent?"

"The question has no answer. There are millions of Indians. Any statement about what they value is a mere generalization. Only individuals value things. They say Indians value their dignity. Who doesn't? I understand their concern may be more acute because the fate they have suffered in the last five hundred years is demoralizing in the extreme. But I also value dignity, and when a university tribunal ordered me to attend sensitivity training offered by a charlatan Indian activist from Colorado, I resigned."

His shoulders slumped down slightly. "It was not an act of great courage. The fact was that I no longer wanted to work among the new faculty schooled in the radical graduate programs of the sixties."

He took another sip of water. "Empathy is not my strong suit. I was taught that the best thing an anthropologist can do is study cultures and report on them as a scientist. The worst thing you can do is give them sympathy. They don't want it, and it clouds your objectivity. The new faculty didn't see Native American culture as something to be studied. They saw it as a cause. Maybe their view had some merit I failed to grasp . . ."

His voice trailed off and his head angled down. Then he looked up at me. "At any rate, I tried not to look back when I left. Then this summer a very old friend of mine from the San Roque Pueblo came to see me."

"San Roque!"

"Yes. Many of the rumors about them are either false or exaggerated. I lived among them for a year during a sabbatical. My friend, Otaku Ma'sin, was very old and wanted to unburden himself. He told me he had heard about the University returning artifacts to the Indians. He believed the University had a collection of very old Ma pots. They call themselves the Ma people. 'San Roque' is obviously the name the Spaniards gave them. The pots have never been returned."

"Why did he think telling you would unburden him?"

"Because there was a tribal elder whose position would have made him the designated recipient on behalf of the Ma, and when the pots were never placed in their kiva where they belonged, Otaku at first believed the elder had kept them for himself."

"And he changed his mind?"

"Yes. He and the elder were alone one evening in a field of corn, and Otaku saw a yellow glow around the elder. This is a sign of purity. So Otaku figured the pots never got to the Pueblo. He was hoping I might right the wrong. He was also hoping his delay in reporting the absence of the pots would not become what the Ma call a scar on his soul."

"Did you ever see anyone glowing yellow during the year you lived there?"

"Of course not. But I don't question Otaku's judgment of the

THE POT THIEF WHO STUDIED PTOLEMY

elder any more than I question my wife's judgment of you. The fact that he saw purity in the elder I accept. If it manifested itself as a yellow glow, then put it down to cultural conditioning. Or the reflected rays of the setting sun off the corn. At any rate, I believe the pots never found their way to San Roque."

"And I take it you have a theory about what happened to them."

"I do. And you are correct to call it a theory. I would not like you to give it any more credence than the word implies. I believe Ognan Gerstner stole them."

And that is why, three days later, I found myself downtown staring at Rio Grande Lofts.

5

What did I see?

An eleven-story building with few means of ingress. Since it was originally built for offices, it had no balconies you could scale. The front door on the east side of the building opened to a lobby attended twenty-four hours a day by doormen. Two security cameras were visible through the plate glass, one pointed at the front door and one at the two elevators.

A service entrance on the west side of the building was secured by a lock that could be opened only from the inside. I determined that by walking up to the door and noticing there were no knobs or keyholes in it.

On the south side of the building, a ramp led to a basement parking garage. The opening at the top of the ramp was somewhat larger than the average garage door, maybe ten feet wide and eight feet tall, and was protected by a gate that came within an inch or two of the concrete on the bottom, top and both sides. A snake might slip between the gate and the surrounding concrete while the gate was closed, but a jackrabbit couldn't.

The gate was constructed of vertical iron bars six inches apart. I determined that by walking up to the gate and measuring. I could not see any security cameras. A metal column near the left wall held a keypad. Residents entered by punching in a code and waiting for the gate to slide open.

Twenty feet to the left of the garage entrance was a garage exit. It had the same sort of gate, except there was no keypad. The exit gate opened automatically when a car approached it from inside the garage.

I assumed there was a door on the roof, so I decided to start my analysis at the top of the building.

But first I walked down the street to a drugstore and purchased a magazine. I can't remember the last time I bought a magazine, and I was surprised by how expensive they've become. Since I had no plans to read the magazine, I selected the one with the lowest price. It was called Chrome Hogs and sold for $2.95.

I took the magazine back to a bus stop across from the garage entrance where I sat on the bench pretending to read. What I was actually doing was examining the building and thinking about how I might gain entrance.

At least that's what I started to do. But when I removed the plastic wrapper and opened the magazine, I discovered it was full of motorcycles adorned by exotic women in various states of undress. I don't know what pornography is, but—like Justice Potter Stewart—I know it when I see it.

And this was not it. There is nothing prurient about a woman leaning over a Harley and wearing a tank top that reveals tattoos on her breasts of little spigots that say "chocolate" on the left and "vanilla" on the right.

I shifted my eyes from the glossy pages to the roofline across the street. Tall buildings have doors to access the rooftop machinery—chillers, compressors, pumps, monkey wrenches or whatever they have up there. If I could get on the roof, I could probably get into the building.

There was no fire escape or exterior staircase. Of course I could reach the roof via the interior staircase, but I would already have to be inside to do that, wouldn't I? Renting a helicopter didn't merit much consideration. No tall buildings loomed next to Rio Grande Lofts, so I couldn't leap across from one roof to the other like a movie stunt man or secure a rope between them or anything of that sort. Even if those things had been possible, I wouldn't have attempted them. I'm severely acrophobic.

I was checking the roof entrance off the list of possibilities when a woman with a small child and a large shopping bag plopped down next to me. I could see why she preferred riding a bus to walking. She had the physique of the Michelin man, but she lacked his pleasant smile. She gasped for breath and yelled, "Sit still, Kyle, and stop tormenting me."

She didn't look or sound like the sort of mother little Kyle obeyed, and little Kyle didn't look like he ever sat still. But to my amazement, he did just that. He became quiet. He stared in my direction. I followed his line of vision and discovered why. He had zeroed in on *Les Grand Tetons*.

Then the Michelin woman saw what he was looking at. She jerked little Kyle off the bench, slung her shopping bag against me, and huffed away.

I'm five feet six and weigh one hundred and forty pounds. Her shopping bag had approximately the same dimensions, and it almost knocked me off the bench.

The magazine fell to the sidewalk and opened to another page with a picture of a motorcycle with huge saddlebags and a zaftig woman astride the seat with equally large appendages. I decided I had seen all I needed to see of Rio Grande Lofts. And of *Chrome Hogs.* I threw the magazine in the trash and continued my analysis on the walk home.

I could drive through the garage entrance if I had a code. I could walk through without a code by following a car, but the driver would surely spot me and call security. I couldn't linger until the car was out of sight in the garage and then run in. I had been on the bench long enough to see some cars come and go, and the gates on both the entrance and exit operated swiftly and efficiently.

If I ran in through the exit gate when someone drove out, they could still call security, but at least they wouldn't be in the basement with me. But there was a serious flaw with that option. The idea of running down a narrow concrete canyon while an average American motorist—probably with cell phone to ear—drove up that same ramp had me imagining being crushed between car and concrete.

There might be a way to force open the service entrance from the outside, but the only methods that came to mind (a jackhammer, a cutting torch, dynamite) all failed to meet the condition of a surreptitious entry.

The easiest way in was the only one I hadn't considered—through the front door. I had walked only a block or two, so I turned back to try it. I took up a casual but determined pace, assumed an expression of confidence and strode through the front door. I got two steps in before a burly doorman in a maroon blazer with a nametag that read 'Rawlings' stepped in front of me.

"May I help you, sir?"

"I'm here to see Warner Oland."

"We have no resident by that name, sir."

"Are you certain? Maybe he just moved in. Could I see the list of residents?"

"No, sir. Our residents value their privacy. And I assure you we have no Mr. Oland here."

"I'm sure there's some mistake," I persisted. "I even have his phone number. Can I use your lobby phone to call him? Maybe he'll come down and vouch for me."

"Sir," he said politely but firmly, "no one enters this building unless a resident is here to receive him. We have no Mr. Oland. I'm afraid I'll have to ask you to leave."

He had the sort of voice you expect to hear saying, "Step away from the building and keep your hands in plain sight." Probably a former cop.

I started home again. If the other doormen were like Rawlings, getting past the front door was unlikely.

6

Emilio Sanchez was outside my door. He removed his hat as I approached.

"Buenos dias, Señor Uberto."

"Buenos dias, amigo," I replied. After we shared an *abrazo*, I asked him, *"¿Ingles o español?"*

"English, of course. Your Spanish, it is too good for me," he said with a wide smile.

"You just like to show off your English. It gets better every time I hear you."

"A man is never too old to learn."

"That is true. How is *Señora Sanchez?*"

"Consuela continues to have the problems of her kidneys, but she sees the doctor and prays to the Virgin."

"And she remains strong?"

"Yes, *gracias a Dios*. Of course, I do the cleaning, but she still like to cook."

"Emilio, Consuela is the best cook in New Mexico. She fed me for eighteen years and you for even longer, and neither one of us grew fat. How do you explain it?"

"It is a miracle."

"I believe it is. And I believe you may have brought some of her food, because a delicious smell is wafting from that bag."

"¿Que quiere decir 'wafting'?"

"It means to be carried on the wind, like the scent of flowers or the smell of food."

"It is a good word, wafting. I will use it when I return to Consuela. *'Querida Consuela,'* I will call to her, 'your perfume was wafting from the house when I arrive on the bus'."

"She is a fortunate lady."

"It is I who am fortunate, my friend. But even so, the doctor, he is very expensive. Every day we give thanks to God for your parents who buy for us the insurance."

"You have a bill for me."

"I am sorry to trouble you—"

"It is no trouble. Since my parents died, I administer their estate, so you must let me handle all the papers from the doctors."

"So you have told me many times, and yet I feel it is much work for you."

"Doing what my parents wanted is never work."

"You are a good—"

"Emilio!"

"Yes?"

"Are you going to show me what's in the bag or are you going to make me starve?"

He beamed and opened the bag. Then he unbent the tin foil to reveal a mound of roasted *cabrito*.

"My favorite. *Muchisimas gracias.*"

Consuela Saenz (she didn't become Consuela Sanchez until I was in college) was our housekeeper and cook, but to me she was like a second mother. She joined our household shortly after I did. My parents said she spoke little English. She spoke Spanish to me, so I grew up bilingual. After I started school, I helped her with her English.

She knew nothing of American food. Oh blessed ignorance! We ate *cabrito, carne adobo, chiles rellenos, fideos, flautas, posole, pollo en mole* and *sopa de lima.* Until I started school, I assumed these were normal fare. The school cafeteria disabused me of that notion. After the first week, I started carrying a sack lunch.

We would have talked longer but Emilio was anxious to return to Consuela. I offered to drive him, but as usual he wouldn't hear of it, so I walked him to the bus stop and waited with him until the bus arrived.

7

The closest bus stop is on Central (aka Route 66) unless you want to get on the silly trolley the city runs through Old Town. In the first place, it's not a trolley because it doesn't run on rails. It's a bus with a gas-guzzling engine under a trolley-looking body. In the second place, it doesn't go where Albuquerqueans want to go. It's really just for tourists.

We once had trolleys powered by electricity. They ran on rails from 1904 to 1927. Well, they didn't run continuously for 23 years, but they did operate on some sort of schedule during those years. Then they were replaced by buses. The same thing happened in New Orleans. Most of their streetcars were replaced by buses, one of which is called *Desire*. Fortunately, there was still a streetcar on Desire Street when Tennessee Williams was writing.

As I walked back from Central, the scent of burning leaves was in the dry, crisp air, and there was a spring in my step and a song in my heart. The tune was *Cow Cow Boogie*. It was being sung by Ella

Fitzgerald and I was humming along. The source of this *joie de vivre* was not only the beautiful New Mexico fall, but also the delicious *cabrito* awaiting me.

Then I turned the corner and saw Miss Gladys Claiborne with a covered dish between her hands and a large canvas bag hanging from her right forearm. In addition to running the eponymous Miss Gladys' Gift Shop two doors west of the shop I own and one door west of the shop I rent, she has a second career trying to fatten me up and marry me off. I told her Emilio had left me a bag of roasted goat.

"Then it's a good thing I brought this King Ranch Chicken," she proclaimed. "Why, just the thought of eating a goat would be enough to put a man off his feed. That Mr. Sanchez seems like such a nice person, but I do declare those Mexicans will eat just about anything. Why, they even put tripe in their stew, and those chile peppers are so hot it's a wonder they don't all have ulcers."

I've found it's better not to argue with Miss Gladys, a name she evidently was known by even during the years of her marriage to the late Mr. Claiborne.

"What is King Ranch Chicken?"

She drew herself up to her full five two. "Are you going to stand there and tell me you've never had King Ranch Chicken?"

"Uh—"

"You need to open that door, Mr. Schuze. I swear this dish is about to get the better of me."

I opened the door, took the dish from her, and placed it on my counter. The bag I recognized from her stock. Fashioned from sturdy canvas with blue check gingham trim, it featured an embroidered picture of the Old Town gazebo on its side. She extracted a placemat, napkin and three pieces of cutlery wrapped in a strip of the same fabric tied in a bow. Then she pulled out a big yellow dinner plate, a matching salad plate, a large glass tumbler and a thermos. It was like watching clowns come out of a Volkswagen.

I was admiring the beautiful glaze on the plate when she produced yet another instrument from the bag—a large silver serving spoon—and covered the plate with the casserole. I began to think the name "King Ranch" must derive from the size of the servings. I admit it smelled good, so I took a tentative taste while she told me about it.

"You melt a stick of butter in your frying pan and cook up a couple of diced bell peppers and a couple of diced onions—Vidalia are the best. Then you put in a package of chicken tenders. When they begin to brown, you pour it all in an ovenproof casserole and add two cans of condensed cream of mushroom soup, two cans of condensed cream of chicken soup and two cans of RO-TEL tomatoes with green chiles. Use the mild—you don't want it to burn like Mexican food. Then you tear up a dozen tortillas into bite-sized pieces, stir it all together with three packages of shredded cheddar cheese and throw it in the oven. Just take it out any time after it starts bubbling and before the cheese starts to look like leather," she said and laughed. She went on to emphasize that you must use RO-TEL brand tomatoes and green chiles. Anything else and it wouldn't be King Ranch.

"Why, it's easier than falling off a log," she averred.

Of course it is, I thought to myself. You don't have to measure since all the ingredients come portioned out in standard quantities such as cans, packages, etc. I did wonder what part of the chicken is its tender. I admit the dish tasted good, although I couldn't stop thinking of all the salt in those canned soups. Fortunately, the thermos held sweetened tea. I drank three glasses to offset the salt.

As I approached the last of the food on my plate, I became increasingly wary of the empty salad plate. I was pretty sure there would be no salad. Miss Gladys doesn't hold with the strange notion of the French that salad can be served after the main course. I suspected dessert, and I didn't think I was up to it. Then she reached in the bag (I looked around to see if perhaps there were two bags and I hadn't noticed one of them) and came up with a plastic storage container packed with peach cobbler. Everyone in Old Town calls Miss Gladys *Nuestra Señora de los Casseroles*. We say it fondly, but not to her face. If Campbell's ever goes out of business, Miss Gladys's cookbook will be rendered useless. But the woman can make cobblers to die for, which was what I feared I might do after I ate the thing.

8

I waddled over to Dos Hermanas a couple of hours later, and Susannah told me I looked a little green around the gills.

"What does the word 'RO-TEL' mean to you?" I asked.

"It's a brand of canned tomatoes with green chiles in it. There must be a case of those cans in my mother's pantry. Why do you ask?"

"I think the RO-TEL company invented a dish called King Ranch Chicken, of which I have just eaten far too much."

"Uh, oh. Miss Gladys?"

I nodded.

"I take it you're skipping dinner tonight."

Another nod.

"You want an Alka Seltzer to drop in your Margarita?"

I pulled a face and took a sip. No matter how full you are, there's always room for alcohol.

"You know what you were doing on Monday at Rio Grande Lofts, Hubie? You were casing the joint," she announced proudly.

"I guess I was," I admitted. "Why do you suppose it's called *casing*?"

"Because you're looking just in case?"

"Hmm."

"This is so exciting, like that old movie on late night television with Humphrey Bogart and that other fat guy."

"Sydney Greenstreet. But Humphrey Bogart wasn't fat."

"I didn't say he was."

"You said, 'Humphrey Bogart and that other fat guy'."

"I meant the guy you mentioned the other day, Warner Oberon."

"His name was Oland, not Oberon."

"I thought maybe he was related to Merle Oberon. I adore her."

"What movies was she in?"

"Wuthering Heights."

"I hope the movie was less boring than the book. What else was she in?"

"The Scarlet Pimpernel," she said and got a puzzled look on her face. "What's a pimpernel?"

"I have no idea." I pressed my upper lip against my teeth and said, "You wanted to say something about Bogart, sweetheart?"

"That doesn't sound like him at all, Hubie. And it's the other guy I wanted to say something about—the fat character. He was the mysterious character who wanted the malted falcon."

"I think that's 'Maltese' falcon."

"Hmm. I thought maybe it was like a giant malted milk ball in the shape of a bird. What does Maltese mean?"

"It means it's from Malta."

"The island in the Mediterranean?"

"Yep."

"Why did they call it that? The whole film takes place in California. Aren't there falcons in California?"

She took a sip of her margarita and shook her head. "Forget the bird. But you understand what I was saying, right?"

Strangely enough, I did. "I think so. Kasper Gutman was a mysterious character trying to get the Maltese falcon, and I'm a mysterious character trying to get the San Roque pots."

"Who's Kasper Gutman?"

"He's the character played by Sydney Greenstreet."

"That's funny, a fat guy playing someone named Gutman. But you can't play a fat guy—you'd have to play the thin man."

"That was William Powell."

"Who cares? It's still exciting. What's your next move?"

I looked around Dos Hermanas and realized how much I enjoyed being there. And how much I would miss it if I were in jail. "Maybe I should forget the whole thing."

"Why?"

"Because the building has professional security, and I'm an amateur burglar."

"Amateur? What about all those pots you've stolen over the years?"

"They were in the ground, not in a building. It's a lot easier. And besides, I didn't steal them."

She gave me her mischievous smile, a little wider than the enigmatic one and a couple of watts brighter. "What do you call it, then?"

"I prefer to think of it as harvesting the riches of the earth. Sort of like prospecting, except for pots rather than gold. Anyone resourceful enough to dig up the pots should get to keep them."

"What about someone resourceful enough to steal them out of a high security building?"

"I'm not sure that would be stealing either," I ventured.

"You're not going to tell me the pots in Gerstner's apartment are part of the riches of the earth are you?"

Perhaps I colored slightly. "Well, they aren't like other things in people's houses."

"No?"

"No. If I burgled a house and took someone's silverware, that would be stealing. But Gerstner stole the pots. He doesn't own them. I don't think I'd feel guilty about taking them."

"Sort of like you felt last spring when you stole that pot from the museum."

"I didn't steal it. And anyway, you know how I feel about archaeology museums. They're places where—"

"I know," she interrupted, "places where pots go to die."

"Well, it's true. Archaeologists call people like me 'pot thieves'. They want exclusive control of every artifact under the ground, and museums are their allies. But you told me yourself that only a small percentage of all the artifacts dug up by archaeologists are actually on display in museums. Most of the stuff is in boxes in the basement either because there's no room to display it or because it's waiting to be studied."

"Yeah. I learned that in our class on deaccessioning."

I winced at the word as much as at the idea. I have a decent vocabulary from all my reading, but I'm not particularly good at language. I never can remember the difference between a simile and a metaphor, and I forget which conjunctions coordinate and which subordinate and don't care anyway. But I know a phony word when I hear one. A curator made up 'deaccession' because saying they deaccessioned some artifacts sounds better than saying they threw them away.

"They rebury most of it, but some of it they toss out," she admitted.

"And they don't want treasure hunters to dig up what they reburied!"

"That's because you don't do it scientifically. You know, measure how deep it was, what sort of seeds were in the petrified poop next to it and all that stuff."

"That's what they claim. But they'll never be able to scientifically dig and study even a small fraction of what's out there, so why hoard things they'll never find? More sites are destroyed by construction in a day than treasure hunters can dig up in a decade. Archaeologists should thank us since we increase the number of artifacts that are saved."

"But you don't put them in museums where they'll be safe."

"Safe from what? Being enjoyed?"

"Okay, suppose I grant your point about museums. What does that have to do with Gerstner's apartment?"

"Well, all we have to do is figure out whether the pots in Gerstner's apartment—if he has them—are like someone's silverware or more like pots in a museum."

"Is this a trick question?"

"Maybe so. Maybe I'm just rationalizing. Anyway, it's probably moot anyway. Staring at Rio Grande Lofts from the bus bench didn't fill me with confidence."

"That reminds me. You know the magazine you bought so you could sit on the bench and look at the women with big boobs?"

"I didn't buy it for that reason. I didn't even know what was in it."

"Yeah, right. Anyway, you know the one with spigot tattoos?"

"Yes."

"Well, it reminds me of an artwork we studied in class. It's a large sculpture of a reclining woman. It's so large you can actually

42

walk inside her body. You enter between the legs of course. And guess what's inside?"

"Digested corn chips?"

"No, a milk bar. You can actually order milk at a bar inside the sculpture of a reclining woman. Isn't that a great concept?"

"You're making this up."

"I'm not. It's actually a famous piece. It's called *Hon-en Katedral*. I think it means 'woman as cathedral'. The artist is Niki de Saint-Phalle."

"I've never heard of her."

"Well, she's famous. There's a perfume named after her."

"That's the mark of a great artist all right."

"Is that sarcasm, Hubert?"

"It is. 'Saint-Phalle' sounds French. Is this cathedral woman in Paris?"

"Nope—Stockholm."

"No doubt right next to Warner Oland's childhood home," I quipped.

She ignored that.

9

I picked up Walter Masoir the next morning in my 1985 Bronco. I needed to talk to someone at San Roque to find out what I would be looking for if I ever got inside Rio Grande Lofts, and Masoir had agreed to get me in the Pueblo.

"Thanks for driving," he said.

"It's the least I could do, especially since I'm the one who wants to go."

His mustache crept up slightly. "But you want access only because I asked you to recover the pots."

I turned and looked at him.

"All right, I didn't ask you. Not in so many words. But it's obvious I would not have shared my suspicions with you had I not expected you to act on them."

"I'd like to see San Roque even if I did nothing about the missing pots."

"What anthropologist wouldn't? But I'm also sure you want to do something about the pots."

He was right, of course. I wanted those pots, partly because I didn't want Gerstner to have them, partly because I wanted to see them, and partly because I thought there was a lot of money to be made. But I was still wavering about actually trying to break in to a building.

Of course you already know what I finally decided. I wouldn't have brought the whole thing up if I hadn't ended up in the damn place.

"It's also good you drove. My only vehicle is a 1965 Chrysler Imperial with a ground clearance of four inches. It would never make it across the ford. This vehicle, on the other hand, seems ideally suited to the task."

"Is the road that bad?"

"It isn't a road. The Jemez flows mostly below ground during half of the year. The wet sand is impassable. But San Roque is situated by a stone outcropping that serves as a ford. The ground there is solid but very bumpy. A few years ago I would have walked, but now . . ." He stared out the window.

"I'll get us across, and you get us in."

He nodded.

San Roque Pueblo is tucked against the mesa on the north side of the Jemez River. On a sunny day, the barren ground resembles a sand painting with its mineral-laden soil displaying hues from mustard yellow to deep magenta. That particular autumn day was cloudy and cold, and the land across the river had the shape and color of elephant skin.

The ford challenged us as Masoir had promised. I nudged the

Bronco across slowly and carefully, but still bottomed out several times to the accompaniment of loud clangs.

We emerged onto a sandy bank surrounded by a dozen men who hadn't been there when we started across. They stood with hands in their pockets, shoulders hunched against the cold. Some looked down, some off to the horizon. None of them looked at us.

Masoir told me to stop the car, turn off the engine and do nothing else. We sat in silence for perhaps three minutes before one of the men started walking to the Pueblo. The others continued to stand in silence. After twenty minutes or so, an old man came down the path and up to the passenger side of the Bronco. Masoir rolled down his window, and the old Indian spoke to him in a language that sounded like one of the Tanoan group. I wasn't knowledgeable enough to tell which one it might be.

Masoir answered. The old man stood there for a while. Finally, he spoke again. Masoir exited the truck and motioned me to follow. Once we had gone a few paces, all the men fell in silently behind us.

As our entourage walked up the trail to the pueblo, I realized it had grown colder, and I wished I'd worn a heavier jacket. We passed corrals and outbuildings and entered an open area between two groups of low-lying adobe structures. Playing children scampered out of sight as we approached, a mongrel dog with a piece of bread in his mouth trotting behind them.

We turned to the west and ducked through a door so low even I had to bend down to enter. We were in a vestibule, dark and devoid of furnishings, with three doors, one straight ahead and one to each side. The old man opened the door on the right and gestured for us to enter. He stayed outside and shut the door behind us.

A piñon fire warmed, lit and perfumed the room. Blankets covered the dirt floor around the logs, and an ancient man sat near the fire in faded jeans, a chambray shirt and a wool sweater a size or two too small.

We sat down opposite him and waited. He looked at me for what seemed like several minutes but was probably only twenty seconds. I tried to return his gaze with as noncommittal a look as I could muster.

He spoke to Masoir briefly. Masoir merely nodded.

A young man entered from a door behind our host and brought us each a bowl of red stew. The old man took a bite, chewed and then signaled for us to eat. The stew had chunks of beef, coarse ground cornmeal, onions, tomatoes and enough dried and ground red chile to incinerate an acre of forest. I finished the bowl as decorum required. Between the log fire and the stew, I was no longer cold.

We lowered our bowls and listened to the Indian speak for perhaps fifteen minutes. I recognized a word or two, not even enough to tell what the topic was, but mostly I enjoyed the sibilant consonants that sounded like dry leaves chased by the wind across sandy ground.

When he finished speaking, he and Masoir exchanged sentences for another ten minutes. Then the old man smiled and fell silent.

10

Masoir was quiet as we rocked and bumped across the river and then plowed through sand up onto the highway. I was concentrating on choosing a path and steering, but my frontal lobe was questioning one of Schuze's Anthropological Premises, abbreviated SAP, which some of my friends say is what you have to be to believe them. The one I was reconsidering was Number 9: Paleolithic cultures will eventually disappear. It's just a matter of time and technology until the aboriginal peoples of the Amazon, for example, will be overrun by so-called civilization. But the Ma were overrun four hundred years ago and were gamely holding on.

When we reached the false security of smooth pavement, Masoir began to tell me what he had learned. The man we ate with had been next to Otaku Ma'sin in the tribal hierarchy. The story of the pots was not one the Ma often shared with outsiders, but the old man—whose name was Sema Ma'tin—knew from Otaku that he could trust Masoir.

Masoir turned to face me. "I may have misled you, Mr. Schuze, and if so I apologize. I didn't realize how much of the Ma language I have lost over the last twenty years. I didn't understand much of what Sema said, and the part I did understand may not be useful to you."

"Please call me Hubert. And I'll be grateful for any information you gathered."

"Well, let me start with one thing I am sure about. There were two sets of pots."

I turned to him with a quizzical look.

"Actually, there have been more than two sets in the past. Ma legend says their ancestors without names made the first set. They attribute great power to the pots."

"Who are the ancestors without names?"

"The Ma divide history more or less as we do with ancient and modern. Their dividing line is based on names they remember. Ma children are taught to recite their ancestors' names back for ten generations. Everyone before that is called an ancestor without a name."

"So all we know about the age of the first pots is that it was more than ten generations ago, say two hundred and fifty years or so."

"Yes, but given the role they play in their culture, they must be much older. Ma'tin said the Spanish stole the first set from them. They crafted a replacement set. That set was stolen by a governor when this area was part of Mexico. They made another set after that."

"Then what?"

"Then the Mexican-American War resulted in New Mexico becoming a U.S. territory. Fearing they were going to be robbed once again, they crafted a duplicate set—that's why I said there were two sets—and they put both sets in the kiva, the new pots in plain sight and the old set hidden. In case the Americans came to steal pots, the Ma hoped they would take the new ones and not know the difference."

I thought how my own copies had fooled people over the years and felt a sudden kinship with the Ma. "Did it work?"

"Yes and no. I'll tell you what I already knew and what Ma'tin told me. First, what I know. The new American administration wasn't interested in stealing pots, so we'll never know if the Ma plan would have worked. What the new administration was interested in was reorganizing the territory. They had surveys made of the pueblos."

"There had never been surveys before?"

He shook his head. "Both the Spaniards and the Mexicans took whatever land they needed, but other than that, they went along with the informal boundaries recognized by the tribes. The stated purpose of the surveys was for official record-keeping, but some of the pueblos complained they ended up smaller after the survey."

"Why am I not surprised?"

"What Ma'tin told me is they lost their kiva to the Americans. I suppose it fell outside the lines of the new survey."

"How could that be? The kiva is in the middle of the village."

Masoir shook his head. "At some point in the distant past, they moved their dwelling area a few miles to the south. As you know, many of the pueblo tribes have done this over the years, sometimes to better defend themselves from the raids of the nomadic tribes, sometimes for superstitious reasons. Anyway, they moved, but they continued to use the primary kiva for ceremonies even though it was no longer in the center of the village. The American survey left the kiva outside their land. When they went to the lost kiva to take the pots and other sacred objects back to their village, they found the kiva had been emptied. All the copies were gone, but some of the originals were hidden well enough not to be found. The Ma still have eight of them."

"How many were taken?"

"Five. Each set contained thirteen pots, one for each lunar month of the year, each bearing a design appropriate to that month."

"So they're missing eighteen pots."

"Yes, but it's only the five originals they want back. For some reason, they consider those pots to carry the same magic as the very first ones."

"And the copies lack magic?"

He nodded.

"Did he tell you what the thirteen designs are?"

"No, but he gave me an example. The pot for the tenth lunar month has a corn design because it's the month of the harvest."

"No other examples?"

"No. I know it would have been helpful for you to have a complete description of the entire set, but he didn't offer, and it would have been inappropriate to ask."

I didn't want to question Masoir's judgment. After all, he was to my knowledge the only white man who had ever lived among the Ma.

I asked him why he'd never seen the pots while they were in the University's possession.

"They were a late addition to the collection, acquired only a year or so before I left. Gerstner kept them under lock and key because he said it would insult the Indians to have white men studying them. I was surprised he accepted the collection, but in retrospect, I think he did so to further his repatriation scheme. The provenance of those pots was shaky to say the least, so everyone wanted to return them to the Ma, myself included. And once you decide that, why not do the same for the other tribes? I explained why not, but to no avail."

"If he really feels that way about artifacts, why would he have kept them himself?"

"Remember, I'm not certain he did. But I know they didn't get back to San Roque, and I personally think Gerstner is a complete phony. He feigned belief in repatriation of artifacts only because that view would best advance his career."

"Well, I think I'll be able to recognize the pots if I see them."

"Ma'tin did tell me the pots are all the same size and use the same color scheme. He even told me the three colors. One of the colors is black, but I didn't recognize the other two color words he used."

"Probably shades of what we would call charcoal and sienna," I guessed.

"You're the potter. I remember color words that were frequently used, like yellow and black. But I doubt I ever knew the words for charcoal or sienna."

"How big are they?"

"Two hands high and one-and-a-half hands across."

"Anything else?"

"Yes. They are made with melting stone."

"What is melting stone?"

"I thought you might know. Some kind of clay?"

"Not that I've heard of."

"Do potters ever use lava? That might be called melting stone."

"Some of the black-on-black pots do use ground pumice—that might be it. Anything else?"

"Just that they want them back because they are amulets. If they have them, their treasure is protected."

"What treasure could they possibly have?"

"Treasure is my loose translation of a Ma word that means something like esteemed or valued. Remember, I'm hardly an expert."

"You may be the only white man who understands their language. You're my expert until someone better comes along."

"Maybe the treasure is something abstract like luck," Masoir speculated.

"They don't seem to have enjoyed much luck," I commented.

He was staring out across the river as we approached Albuquerque. "Do you know who San Roque was?"

I shook my head.

"I know only because I was curious as to why the Spaniards chose that name, so I looked it up. Roque was born in the thirteenth century. Tradition says he had a birthmark in the form of a red cross on his chest. He was from a wealthy family. When his parents died, he gave all his money to the poor and joined the Franciscan order. As a monk, he devoted himself to caring for the victims of the plague. He is said to have contracted the disease. He made a miraculous recovery and went on to perform many miracles of healing. After his death, he became the patron saint of plague victims."

"So the Spanish named the Ma Pueblo 'San Roque' because the Indians had the plague?"

"That's the story they gave. The Ma think the plague came upon them because the pots were stolen."

"What do you think?"

"I don't believe in amulets, theirs or ours. The pots didn't help the Ma, and Roque's cross didn't help him."

"How so?"

"He was arrested as a spy by his uncle who didn't recognize him. He died in prison. When they were preparing to bury him, they found the birthmark, and only then did his uncle realize he had kept his nephew in prison until he died."

11

"I can't believe you actually visited San Roque. It looks so bleak, and you hear all those stories. There's not even a bridge. How did you get there?"

"The river bottom there is rocky, so you just drive across."

"And how did the old wreck do on the rocks?"

"He rode it out with no complaint. The Bronco also did well."

"Not nice, Hubie."

"I like the old guy. His mind is sharp, and he commands respect from the Ma."

"So you think you'll be able to recognize the pots?"

"Probably. Although knowing the colors would make it easier. The old man told us all three colors, but Masoir didn't know the Ma words for two of them."

"Why didn't he ask them for the English words? Don't they speak English out there?"

"I'm sure some of them do. They just choose not to."

"So you'll be trying to burgle something you may not even recognize?"

"I'll recognize them. I know the size, I know what is probably the dominant color and I know something else."

"What?"

"Gerstner isn't a pot collector. So any pot I find in his place will almost certainly be one of the missing Ma pots."

"What will you do with them if you find them?"

I thought it over while I sipped my margarita. Before my trip to San Roque, I would have said I'd sell most of the pots to a discriminating collector and keep one for myself to admire. Now that I knew the history of the pots—or at least part of it—I wasn't so sure. I felt like I had a duty to return any of the originals I found and sell only the copies. The copies were genuine Ma pots after all, and a collector wouldn't know or care what the Ma thought about their lack of magic.

"Maybe the pots will tell me."

"I know pots have mouths, but I don't think they talk. And anyway, they'd probably speak Taos."

"Tanoan. Actually, Tanoan is a group of languages, like Slavic or Romance."

"Well, I don't speak any of those, especially Romance." She hesitated for a moment, and then said, "I'm thinking of going online."

"I thought you were already online. You tell me about emails you receive. Don't you have to be online to get email?"

"Hubert, talking to you about computers makes me know how you anthropologists must feel when you stumble across a primitive tribe. I'm not talking about email. I'm talking about an online dating service. See, you post your picture and a little write-up about yourself telling prospective dates what you like and don't like, and then if someone is interested, they contact you via the dating service site and the two of you can exchange messages. If you're both interested, you can make plans to meet."

It sounded like the worst idea I'd ever heard, but I tried not to change my expression, and I told myself to keep an open mind. After all, this was the first time I'd ever heard there were online dating services. I figured I should at least hear more about them before writing them off as one more piece of evidence that civilization as we know it is crumbling.

I selected the largest tortilla chip in the bowl, loaded it up with salsa and started chewing.

Susannah looked at me expectantly, but I kept on chewing. "Well, are you going to say anything?"

"Anthropologists don't stumble across primitive peoples. We search them out deliberately."

"I knew you'd hate the idea. I don't know why I told you."

"I don't hate it. I just don't understand it."

"What's not to understand? It's just a blind date, except it's arranged by an online dating service instead of your well-meaning aunt fixing you up with her next door neighbor's son who's a brilliant doctor. Except he turns out to be a pathologist with bad teeth and a comb-over, and the only people he deals with all day are dead. At least an online service screens people and you get to see a picture of them."

"I understand the blind date part, Suze. What I don't understand is why you need to do that. You're attractive, intelligent and have a good sense of humor. Men should be lining up to date you."

"They are, but the line-up looks like one you'd see down at the police station. Of the last three guys I've dated, one turned out to be married, one had a third-grade vocabulary, and the last one's idea of an aftershave was something that smelled like Pine-Sol."

"Maybe if you didn't spend so much time with me—"

"Don't be ridiculous," she snapped. "What sort of a date would I meet at five o'clock? If I don't have a date by five, I'm not likely to meet one during the rush hour."

"Well, I guess that makes—"

"And have I ever hesitated to skip our cocktail hour if I did have a date?"

"No, but—"

"And anyway, Hubert, people don't have to give up friends in order to date. I actually know girls who have lots of friends and lots of dates. I just don't happen to be one of those girls."

"Can I say something?"

"Sure. Nothing's stopping you."

"I think you will have lots of dates. In fact, I know you will. You're just in a bit of a slump. Things will change, and soon your only problem will be deciding which guy to go out with. But if you think an online dating service may get you over this temporary drought, then why not give it a try?"

I felt a little nicer, but I put some more food in my mouth so I wouldn't say anything further on the topic of computer dating.

12

"Your shop next door is closed," said Martin.

"The white man's way," I said, "is to greet people with a salutation."

"Like, 'Hello, we've come from Europe to steal your land'?"

"You're a quick study."

"But you aren't. Your shop next door is still closed."

"This one is open."

"This one is full of fakes."

"I prefer to call them replicas."

"If you can only open one shop at a time, wouldn't it be better to open the one with the expensive stuff?"

"I'm gonna take business advice from someone whose people sold Manhattan for twenty-four dollars worth of beads?"

"Those were the smart ones. The rest of us didn't get a dime, and we gave up the whole damn continent."

Martin Seepu is my height but thirty pounds heavier, all of it muscle. He's clean-shaven, a practical fashion choice since he has only about ten whiskers that need shaving. He has plenty of coarse hair on his head and he wears it in a ponytail.

I first met him when, as an idealistic college freshman, I signed up for a mentoring program the University had created to bring together college kids and children on the reservations. How this was supposed to help the kids on the reservation was never clear to me, but I liked working with Martin. I introduced him to math and he surprised me by liking it.

I started as a math major, but I couldn't see a career path there, and everyone told me I should be an accountant, so I studied that for lack of a better idea. I worked briefly as an accountant after graduating, found it even duller than it sounds and returned to UNM to study archaeology and anthropology.

Martin dropped out of school when he was thirteen, but I'm confident it wasn't a result of my mentoring. He just got tired of condescending teachers covering boring material. Plus, there was less social pressure in his pueblo to finish school than there is outside the reservation. The politically correct opinion is that the dropout rate among Native Americans is a national disgrace. I'm not certain about that. Education is great, but education and schooling are not always the same thing. Martin is a voracious reader and is better educated than most people who have college degrees. He made a decision early on to remain on the reservation, and the life he leads there wouldn't be any different if he had a diploma. It wouldn't enhance his self-esteem, which I always tell him is overdeveloped anyway, and it wouldn't help him get a job because he doesn't want one. He and his extended family raise horses, tend their orchard and garden and work as artisans. His uncle is a potter. Martin works in metal. He works part time in a wrought iron shop in Albuquerque when he feels the need to be in the cash economy for a while.

The Seepus are a close-knit, happy and successful family. Their pueblo, unfortunately, has its share of alcoholism, domestic violence, depression and suicide. Those are the true national disgraces. I don't think more education is the answer, but I don't know what the answer is.

Martin is the only person I know who walks more than I do. His pueblo is nine miles from the edge of town, but he often walks in and back if he has reason to come to Albuquerque. I figured he didn't come in just to tell me my shop was closed. Martin often comes to sell me a pot when his uncle decides to part with one. Sometimes he comes just to visit.

He took the carafe off my coffee maker and poured the coffee in the street. Then he reached in a canvas sack, pulled out a milk jug of water from his pueblo's secret spring and used it to brew a fresh pot. When the gurgling stopped, he poured us both a cup. It was good coffee.

He pulled a pot from the bag and handed it to me.

I spent a long time looking at it and enjoying its heft in my hands. The cloud and lightning motif peculiar to Martin's pueblo ran round its perimeter, but the ratios were different somehow. The base was thicker than normal. The design had a three-dimensional quality I'd never seen before. Potters use several techniques to achieve depth. They can show some objects smaller so they appear to be further away. They can place one object overlapping another so the one overlapped appears to be behind the other. They can achieve depth with color by rendering distant mountains lighter than those in the foreground.

The objects depicted on traditional Native American pottery are flat. They're represented as being on a plane even though the surface of the pot is curved. I can copy that, but I'm not sure I could do it if I were to create a design of my own. The pot Martin brought demonstrated perfectly how a flat plane can be represented on a curved surface, but it still had an elusive, almost invisible sense of depth. I finally decided the glaze where the lightning coincided with the clouds must have been altered ever so slightly. You sensed the jagged lightning behind the cloud even though when you covered everything up except one cloud, it seemed to be of uniform color value.

Finally, I looked up at Martin. "This is the best work your uncle ever did. I'm surprised he's willing to sell it."

"He didn't make it."

"Who did?"

He shrugged.

I held it up to catch the sunlight from the window. The glaze was the key. "I was assuming it was your uncle's because you brought it. But now I see it couldn't be. It was made before he was born. It's not the work of the ancient ones—it's too precise—but it is very old."

"How old?"

"My best guess would be a hundred years, but I could be way off."

"I doubt it. You know your pots pretty good for a yellow hair."

"My hair is brown."

"You all look the same to me."

"Then how come you always recognize me?"

"You're the short one."

"I could point out that you're the same height as me."

"Yeah, but in my tribe, I'm tall."

"Where did you get this?"

"From my uncle."

"Where did he get it?"

"I don't know, but he wanted you to see it."

"Your uncle ever see anything like this before?"

He shrugged again.

I sat the pot down on the corner, suddenly nervous about holding it. "You know what this is worth?"

"Me guess much wampum."

"You guess right, Tonto. At least fifty thousand, maybe twice that much. What does your uncle want me to do with it?"

"I don't know. But don't sell it."

13

Martin calls the pots in my new shop fakes because they are.

I own the east third of a north-facing adobe a block off the square in Old Town. The proceeds from the sale of the pots that got me expelled provided the down payment, and the mortgage has only five years to run.

The middle third of the building became vacant last spring when the former tenant was arrested for murder. If he ever gets out of prison, I'm a good candidate for his next victim. I'm the one who proved he did it.

The owner offered to rent me the space with a five-year option to buy. Maybe I'll accumulate a down payment during the next five years. If not, I can wait until my current mortgage is paid off and take a new one. Meanwhile, I have both a mortgage payment and a rental payment.

My landlord now enjoys not only my rental payments but also depreciation he can take off his taxes. Which just shows you how ridiculous the tax laws are, because the building is definitely not depreciating. It is appreciating and has been doing so steadily for three hundred years. According to the original title, the house was built by Don Fernando Maria Arajuez Aragon when the Spaniards returned after being driven out by the pueblo revolt of 1680. He sold it three years later to Don Pablo Benedicion Verahuenza Orozco for 15 pesetas. I don't know how much 15 pesetas were worth in the late 1600s, but it took a lot of appreciation for the price to climb to the outrageous level I'll have to pay if I decide to exercise my option to buy.

My shop faces north and fronts the street. My living area faces south and fronts the alley. Or should that be 'backs the alley'? My workshop is between the two. Since renting the new space, I had spent most of my time there making copies of the genuine pots in my inventory.

I have a gift. I can reproduce ancient Southwestern Native American pottery. I couldn't duplicate Japanese Raku or the ring vases of Scotland, but if any of my faux Anasazi pots are excavated a hundred years from now, I'm confident they will end up displayed in a museum as the genuine article.

The genuine pots I dig up share shelf space with my clever copies. The ancients didn't sign their pots so I follow their example. I never claim my copies are genuine. I remain silent. *Caveat emptor.*

I once had a buyer who paid with a bad check. Then he had the pot appraised by an expert who told him it was a fake. The appraiser was guessing, but I couldn't argue, could I? I had invested a good deal of time and effort in that pot, but I never got any money for it. *Caveat venditor.*

Despite all my experience with copies, it had never occurred to me until recently that I could sell fakes as fakes. It turns out there's a market for things people know are not the real deal. The fifty dollar Mexican Rolex probably outsells the Swiss model.

So I started making copies of the real pots in my inventory. Some of the older ones are worth anywhere from $10,000 to $50,000. A replica will fetch ten to twenty percent of the price of the original. So people who admire my genuine 1940 Santo Domingo pot but don't want to shell out twenty thousand for it can buy my home-made replica for $3,000. The pot they get is just as beautiful as the original and indistinguishable even down to the brand new patina. You might think 'new patina' is an oxymoron, but if you saw one of my replicas, you would change your mind. I'm sorry I can't tell you how I do it—it's a trade secret.

It's important my replicas look old because, although I hate to think ill of my customers, I suspect some of them don't tell their friends and neighbors their pots are fakes.

Working all summer, I had built up the inventory in my new store. Being a tenant doesn't entitle me to connect the two spaces by cutting through the wall, so I was only opening one at a time, usually the new one. Business is brisker for copies, and if someone wants one of the expensive originals, they know where to find me because I leave a sign to that effect on the door of the original store.

I had forty real pots and a few of my anonymous copies on offer in the store I own. I had ten declared copies displayed in the store I rent. I had made twice that many, but I sold ten copies during the summer for a total take of $24,250. That sounds like a good summer until you realize that the genuine pots I sold during that same summer (a total of two, alas) produced more revenue than the ten copies. Making and selling fake pots is fun and profitable, but I wasn't planning to give up digging for real ones.

My original shop showed the wear and tear of every one of its three hundred years when I bought it. The back portion of the space had been the storeroom. I remodeled it into my living space, coating the walls with adobe plaster. The only seams are two expansion joints. But they aren't there for expansion purposes.

I inserted the expansion joints because when you turn and press the wall sconce to the left of them in a certain way, the plaster panel between the joints swings out on invisible hinges to reveal my secret hiding place.

After Martin left, I deposited the pot he brought there. Then I walked up to the St. Neri gift shop in the former convent next to the Church to see if they had a pamphlet about the saints. I wanted to know more about San Roque. They had the pamphlet and something even better, a colorful carving of San Roque by the famous *santera* Marie Romero Cash. I knew I had to have it when I saw she depicted the Saint with sores on his knees, attended by a dog who was licking those lesions. I knew that scientists had recently discovered that dogs can smell cancer in their masters, and I conjectured that the same must be true for the plague. Then I wondered if the *santeros* of New Mexico knew the power of dogs long before scientists 'discovered' it.

I put the carving on my kitchen table before returning to the new store. I entered from the alley and was helping myself to a second cup of coffee when they came in. It was pretty clear they weren't there to buy pots. They had baseball bats, but I didn't think they were there to play ball either.

As I stood there in shock and fear, two of them started smashing my pots with vicious swings. The third one started towards me.

I believe non-violence is usually the right path, but I am not a total pacifist. There are times when you have to stand up for what is right. Times when you have to disregard your own personal safety and put yourself in harm's way to stop wrongdoing. And, clearly, this was not one of those times.

I ran out the back as fast as my little legs could carry me, dashed the twenty feet to my back door, slammed and locked it, and called 911. Then I sat down at my kitchen table and prayed to San Roque for protection.

14

The police knocked ten minutes later, but it felt like a full hour.

"How do I know it's the police?" I asked through the door.

"Open the damn door, Hubert," replied Whit Fletcher, Detective First Grade, Albuquerque Police Department.

Fletcher wore a shiny silver suit and a spread-collar green shirt with the top button undone. A black string tie lurked under the collar like a shy snake. Fletcher is six feet tall with a slight paunch. His eyes slant downward giving him a hangdog look, and he has wrinkles on his cheeks and a dimple on his chin. He was clean-shaven that day but in need of a haircut. He ran his fingers through his hair to get it off his forehead and said, "You look a little peaked, Hubert."

"What took you so long?"

"It's nice you civilians appreciate us. We got here in record time. You was only cowering in here for ten minutes."

"It seemed longer. And I wasn't cowering. I was hiding."

"From what?"

"From three goons who were smashing up my store and threatening to do the same to me."

"Let's go take a look."

"Are they still there?"

"Yeah, they was thoughtful enough to wait for us so we wouldn't have to put out an APB."

Several caustic responses sprang to mind but went unspoken. I've known Whit for a few years and had more dealings with him than I should have had. He's basically a good cop. I think his gruffness is mostly an act. He's been known to supplement his income when it doesn't significantly divert the flow of justice, but he's hard on the truly bad guys. He's also hard on the King's English and even the plain American version.

I suppose all ten of my replicas had been smashed, but I couldn't be certain because the only things left on the shelves were small fragments and dust. If you break a properly fired clay pot, you get a few large shards. If you smash one of the shards, it breaks into smaller ones. A clay pot does not shatter into small pieces all at once.

The small amount of debris left behind offered no clue as to whether they had broken all the pots or only some of them. And I didn't know which way I wanted it. On the one hand, I wanted the pots to survive. I hadn't put any blood or tears into them, but I had invested a good deal of sweat. On the other hand, I didn't want those crazies to have any of my pots. I knew at least some of the pots had been smashed. But what I really couldn't figure out is why they took the pieces with them?

"Anything missing, Hubert?"

"I would think a trained detective would notice the store is empty."

"No need to get huffy. I figured maybe you only sell stolen pots

70

in this new store, so you keep 'em out of sight. The place could use a good dusting."

"I don't sell stolen pots."

"I don't care if you do so long as they're the ones you dig up. Just don't steal 'em out of people's houses, cause then you'd be a burglar."

"And the dust is from the replicas they smashed."

"What's a replica?"

"It's a copy."

"So you've branched out from selling stolen pots to selling fake ones?"

"Selling fake pots is not illegal."

"Let's let the DA decide that. You wouldn't happen to have picture of these fakes, would you?"

"No, but I have pictures of the pots they were copies of."

"I guess that'll have to do."

"Believe me, Whit, no one can tell the difference."

15

Susannah said, quite reasonably, "I can't understand why they took the broken pots with them."

"Neither can I."

"Did they look like Indians?"

"I think asking if someone looks like—"

"Don't tell me it's politically incorrect to say someone looks like an Indian. I already know that. But you know what I mean. Did they have blue eyes and blond hair like a Swede?"

"Warner Oland was a Swede and he had brown hair and eyes."

"I don't care what he looked like. As far as I'm concerned, he had black hair and slanty eyes."

"That was just the clever Hollywood makeup."

"Hubert, I'm trying to help you here and you keep dragging red herrings across my effort."

"Did you know herrings come from Sweden?"

"Geez. Just forget I brought it up."

"Sorry, Suze. I'm still upset. I don't know what to do, maybe because there's really nothing I *can* do. I started to call and tell you I wouldn't come today, and then I thought what am I going to do, sit around and stew all evening? So here I am, and I really do feel better now that I have you to talk to, but I'm not even doing that right."

"You probably have post dramatic syndrome."

"I think that's post *traumatic* syndrome."

"Well, guys smashing up your shop with baseball bats sounds pretty dramatic to me. Would you rather talk about something else?"

I shrugged.

"I think you'd feel better if we could figure out why those guys smashed your pots. And if we knew why they took the pieces, it might help us understand why they smashed the pots to begin with."

"That sounds good. You wanted to know if the three guys looked like Indians. Well, they had brown skin and black hair."

"So they could have been from the pueblos."

"Yeah. But they could also have been from Chile for all I know."

"Let's assume the pueblos, Hubert. I don't think Chileans would come all the way to Albuquerque to smash your pots."

I nodded in acknowledgement.

"Maybe they thought you were insulting their culture by copying their pots."

"Why wouldn't they come tell me that first and ask me to stop? Their culture puts a premium on conciliation and talking things out. It's not like them to show up and smash things."

"And most environmentalists don't set fire to logging trucks, but any group can have a few crazies."

"Okay, let's say you're right. Why did they take the pieces?"

"So you couldn't put them back together again."

She seemed pleased with that conjecture, and I'll admit it might make sense to someone who isn't a potter. Which is why I hadn't even thought of it.

"Hate to disappoint you, but I couldn't have put those pieces back together even with the help of all the King's horses and all the King's men."

"Well, maybe they wanted to bury the pieces back on Indian land, not let them stay with the white man."

"If they were insulted by the copies, why would they want to bury the pieces on their land?"

"Oh, right. Well, maybe they didn't know they were fakes."

It was like the light bulb going on, but it didn't burn for long. "Now you're getting somewhere. Maybe they didn't know I now have two stores. Maybe they thought they were smashing up the store I've had for many years."

Then I thought about it some more and said, "But that doesn't work, does it? If they thought the pots were originals, they would want to repatriate them, not smash them."

"So they knew they were fake?"

"I think they had to know."

"So we're in a dilemma. If they thought the pots were real, they would have taken them without smashing them. And if they thought they were fakes, they would have smashed them without taking them."

I nodded. She shook her head and waved at Angie, and we got a much-needed refill. Trying to make sense of the pot smashing incident was thirsty work.

"So now what?" she asked.

"Now I break in to Rio Grande Lofts."

"Great!" she almost shouted. Then she tried to restrain herself, which goes against her nature. "I guess I shouldn't say that, huh? I don't want you to get in trouble."

"I'm glad you're enthusiastic about it. I'll need all the moral support I can get. Frankly, the prospect of breaking in to the Lofts scares me."

"Then why do it?"

"I know this sounds crazy, but I'd like to see the pots. I've had this fascination for pots ever since I dug up the ones that got me expelled. After learning about the history of the Ma pots, I'd like to hold them in my hands and copy them."

"You'd risk prison for that?"

"No way. But I would like to return the five missing pots from the older set to the Ma."

"And you would risk prison for that."

I shook my head. "I'm not that noble. I guess it comes down to money."

"What's wrong with that?"

"It makes me a common thief, stealing for money."

"But you're not a thief. You're a good person."

"I try to be. But Consuela's medical bills are costing me a fortune. Now that I've lost half my income, there's no way I can do it. All my copies have been smashed, and I'm paying rent on an empty store."

"But doesn't the insurance pay most of Consuela's medical bills? The deductible and co-pay can't be that high."

I took a sip of my margarita and slouched down in my chair.

Susannah looked me in the eyes. Hers are big and light brown and clear as a perfect agate held up to the desert sun. "There isn't any insurance, is there?"

I shook my head.

"You tell Emilio and Consuela there is insurance, but—"

"Let's not talk about it, Suze."

16

The patio on the east side of my living area is surrounded by an eight-foot wall. Chamisa sprang up against it several years ago. I like the tallow flowers in the spring and straw-like look in the fall. Two cottonwood trees support a hammock, and the final horticultural touch is some native grass growing between the rust-colored flagstones.

The patio also contains some man-made objects. One is a kiva oven my enthusiasm for clay led me to build. I intended to bake bread. After fifty or sixty attempts, I abandoned all hope, but I sometimes light a wood fire in it for warmth. I also have a kiln for firing my pots and two telescopes. Actually, I don't fire the telescopes. I just look through them.

The two scopes serve different purposes. My refractor scope is what you probably think of when you picture a telescope. It's a long thin tube with a lens at one end and an eyepiece at the other. It's good for observing close objects like the moon, the planets, asteroids, and the moons of other planets. It was also great to have when the Hale-Bopp comet passed over in 1996.

The problem with refractor scopes is they don't gather enough faint light to provide a good view of distant galaxies. For that job, I have a Newtonian reflector, a squat looking thing that uses a concave parabolic primary mirror to collect and focus incoming light onto a flat secondary mirror that reflects the image to an eyepiece that sticks out from the side of the tube.

Stargazing is a great hobby for many reasons, but what I like best is how peering into the fathomless night sky calms the nerves and soothes the soul. No matter how great your earthy troubles, they fade into insignificance as you lose yourself in the immensity of space. Perhaps Ptolemy captured the wonder of it all when he said, "When I follow the multitude of the stars in their circular course, my feet no longer touch the earth."

The three Centauri stars—A, B, and Proxima—are the nearest ones to us not counting our own sun. They're four and a half light years away. That's 25,000,000,000,000 miles. Expressed in words, that is twenty-five-thousand-billion miles. Does that mean anything to you?

Me neither. I know intimately how far a mile is. I walk so much that I can tell you within fifty yards when I've covered a mile. I can do the math to convert light years to miles, but the number is so large that I can't get my mind around it.

The Centauri stars are best seen if you're south of about 29 degrees. New Mexico's southern border is around 30 degrees, so we're a bit too far north. A and B are about the size of our sun. Proxima is much smaller and dimmer and can be seen only through a telescope. Chile would be a great place to view the Centauri threesome because of its latitude, clear skies and great observatories.

So far as I know, it has no pot smashers.

I try to restrict my travel to places I can reach and return from in a day, so I'll never travel south of the 30th parallel. If you have the chance to look at our closest stellar neighbors, you'll be looking at light that started out four and a half years ago and is just now reaching earth. To put it another way, if Centauri A burned out at this instant, we wouldn't know it for four and a half years.

If our own sun burned out, we would know it in only eight minutes. Eight minutes compared to four-and-a-half years. That's how much closer we are to our sun than to the other stars.

Our sun will eventually become a red giant and swallow up the planets Mercury, Venus and Earth. Fortunately, that won't happen for about 5 billion years, so there's no need to make any contingency plans at this time.

There are countless stars other than Centauri, of course, and gazing at any one of them from any location makes you realize your own insignificance.

English has borrowed words from many languages over the centuries and is full of spelling rules notable primarily for the number of exceptions. Homonyms are common and so are jokes based on them. Every kid knows a newspaper is black and white and read all over.

Because Spanish is purer than English and also rigidly phonetic, it has few homonyms and few jokes based on them. There is, however, one such riddle Consuela taught me as a child. "¿Cuantas estrellas hay en el cielo?" How many stars are in the sky? The answer is "*Sin cuenta*," which means "without count" but sounds exactly like the word for fifty—*cincuenta*.

Even though the cocktail hour with Susannah had helped calm me down, I was still obsessing over the pot-smashing incident. I fixed myself a light dinner of tacos filled with the last of the Emilio's *cabrito* and washed them down with two bottles of Cerveza Del Mar. Del Mar and Cabana are two new imports from El Salvador. Maybe after they gave up fighting civil wars, they all turned to brewing beer.

After dinner, I was out in my patio scanning the sky at random using my Newtonian and reflecting on the fact that the stars are indeed without count and space is without end. I suppose if I had been using my other scope, I would have been *refracting* on it. Sorry—I couldn't resist.

I did eventually switch to the refractor to check out Mercury. The red planet displays retrograde motion three or four times a year, and this was one of those periods. Of course you can't tell it in one viewing session.

Ptolemy was born around the year 85. Any year with only two digits is a long time ago, but the most amazing thing about him is not when he was born. It's that the system he devised—the circles on circles thing I told you about—still works today. You may think charting the motion of the planets is no big deal. All you'd have to do is just watch and keep a chart of where they are on each date. And people had more leisure time back in the year 85 because they didn't have cell phones and television.

But it wasn't a simple task for Ptolemy because he believed, as did all the learned folks back then, that the heavenly bodies had to travel in circles around the Earth. Why? Because the Earth was considered to be at the center of the universe. And since the circle is the perfect figure and the heavenly bodies are gods, they have to travel in circles.

Most of us today believe don't believe there are multiple gods. We have multiple politicians instead, and—like the Greek gods—they run around in circles and do bad things to ordinary people.

But nothing in the heavens appears to travel in a circle. Ptolemy's genius was to show that by using circles around circles, you can actually create a path that matches the one your eyes see. I think of Ptolemy as the inventor of the first Spirograph. You remember those? It was a sort of drawing toy with a set of plastic gears. The smaller gears fit inside the larger ones and rotated along the circumference of the larger ones. You would put the rings over a piece of paper, put the point of a pencil through a hole in one of the rings then start everything turning. You could make great patterns. Ptolemy showed how circular motion could account for retrograde motion. As I thought about Ptolemy, I heard *The Windmills of Your Mind* playing in my head.

Kepler was born in 1571, still a long time ago but at least it's a date with four digits. He showed you could explain retrograde motion more easily if you assumed the planets orbit in ovals rather than perfect circles. It also helped that he adopted Copernicus' idea that the earth revolves around the sun, but that's another story.

I was marveling at how Ptolemy and Kepler came up with such ingenious ways to explain the strange reversing motion of the planets. I was also marveling at the telescope that allows residents of a speck of dust in a small corner of the universe to see the far reaches of the cosmos.

And that's when I figured out how to get inside Rio Grande Lofts.

17

I walked in to Dos Hermanas the next evening and handed Susannah a dozen blue irises.

"Hubie! You brought me flowers. That's so nice, and they're beautiful. I'll ask Angie for a big glass with some water, and we'll put them on the table."

After she brought the glass of water, Angie left to get our first round of margaritas and Susannah began arranging the flowers.

"How did you know I like irises?"

"I didn't. I picked them because the shade of blue caught my eye."

"That was so nice. I said I never get flowers and you got me some. Of course—no offense—it would be even better if I got them from a handsome new sweetheart, but getting them from my best friend is the next best thing. And you're a very handsome man. I'll bet all the other girls in here think I'm dating a suave older man, and when they look at you, I'll bet they're jealous."

"Older man?"

"Well, you are old enough to be my father. But you don't look it, no wrinkles, no gray hair . . . you don't color your hair, do you?"

"Am I the sort of person who would color his hair?"

"Of course not. But you are the sort of person who brings a girl flowers to cheer her up. And they're so pretty . . . Hubie!" she almost shouted and then glanced around and lowered her voice. "I just realized why you brought me flowers. You used the flower delivery ruse to get into Rio Grande Lofts."

"I didn't, but I might in the future. The flower delivery plan needs some further thought. For one thing, I don't know the names of any of the residents, so who would I tell the doorman the flowers are for?"

"You know Gerstner lives there. You could say they're for him."

"He also knows me. What if the doorman won't let me take the flowers up? If he calls Gerstner to come down to the lobby to get the flowers, I'll be recognized."

She sipped her margarita while she thought about it. Cold air had spilled south out of the Sangre de Cristo Mountains, and there was already some powder on the top of the Sandias. A few hardy folks were on the veranda wearing quilted vests, but Susannah and I had taken refuge at our usual table inside.

"Maybe you don't need a name. After all, you're just the delivery boy, not the person who took the order. You could just say the flowers are for apartment 13."

I shook my head. "There may not be an apartment 13. I don't know the numbering system."

"Then how did you know Gerstner lives in 1101?"

"I looked him up in the phone book."

"Well, there must be a 1001 and a 901 and so on."

"You're probably right, but I think I'll save the flower delivery ruse for back up. I have another way to get in." I told her the plan I'd hatched while stargazing.

"So that's why you're not ordering another margarita?"

"My job sometimes calls for sacrifices."

"Being a burglar isn't a job, Hubert."

"I'm not a burglar, Suze."

She gave me that Mona Lisa smile, and I was glad being a burglar was back on our repartee agenda.

"Don't you get lonely sitting out there all by yourself looking at the stars?"

"You can't be lonely unless you're thinking about yourself. When I look at the stars, I forget everything about myself, so I'm not lonely or sad or anything else."

"I know what you mean. My father says 'A man who's wrapped up in himself makes a very small package'."

"Your father is a wise man."

"He is. When I'm writing about a painting I really like, I can get caught up in it and never give a thought to anything else. Like my non-existent love life. But when I finish the paper, I'm still not dating."

"What about your computer plan?"

I thought she blushed ever so faintly. "I started working on it, but it's harder than I thought it would be. Maybe you can help me."

"I don't think so. You know how little I know about computers."

"The computer part isn't the problem. It's deciding what to put on the site that's hard."

"Like what picture to use?"

"Yes, and what to say about myself."

"That should be easy. Just say you're attractive, intelligent, and too good for any loser looking for a date on a computer."

"I'm looking for a date on the computer."

Oops. "I didn't mean you. I meant the guys."

She stared at me for a few seconds. "You might have the right idea."

"That the guys looking for dates on the computer are losers?"

"No, that I should write something sort of edgy."

"I don't get it."

"See, the problem is I looked at what other people wrote just to get some ideas, and now everything I write sounds like the trite stuff everybody else writes. 'Fun-loving girl seeks adventurous man.' What does that sound like?"

"Like it might be a girl just looking to do the sideways samba."

"Exactly. So to get away from the party girl image, I tried things like 'seeking a mature and caring man in his thirties', and—"

"It sounds like someone shopping for a husband."

"Exactly. So maybe what I need to say is exactly what you suggested."

I gulped. "Even the part about the losers?"

"Especially that part. Someone who would see the humor in that might be just the sort of guy I'm looking for. Someone who doesn't take himself too seriously, someone who's just as worried about going online as I am."

I started getting nervous. "I wasn't being serious. I don't know anything about this whole arena, and I wouldn't want to be responsible for you meeting up with—"

"I'm a big girl. It won't be your responsibility." She waved for Angie. "All of a sudden my enthusiasm for this idea is back, thanks to you."

My enthusiasm for the idea had lessened from where it started, which was zero on the enthusometer. And despite what Susannah said, I knew I would feel responsible if a fiasco resulted from the ad she was determined to place.

It was time for Susannah's class, so she scooped the flowers out of the glass, gave me a peck on the cheek and said, "Good luck tonight."

I was tempted to order another margarita, but I was driving, so I settled for the check instead.

18

Covering the inside of the Bronco's windows with newspaper and masking tape was my first plan—cheap and effective. But also likely to raise suspicion, and you know me—I don't take unnecessary risks no matter how small. So I'd spent most of the afternoon looking for fabric.

I gave no thought in my youth as to where to buy fabric, but I remembered it was available at Sears, so I went there and discovered they no longer sell it. A minor disappointment compared to the discovery they no longer sell candy. I tried the other department stores in the mall with the same luck. No fabric, no candy. I rarely eat sweets, but the childhood memory of the maple nuts at Sears had me looking for some.

There was a kiosk selling candy. Actually, the kiosk was just sitting there. A young lady inside it was selling the candy. She told me they didn't have maple nuts, and she also told me I could buy fabric at Wal-Mart.

She was right. They had the fabric, the greeter was an elderly gentleman who seemed genuinely pleased to see me, and they even had maple nuts, so I bought a package of those as well.

I pinned the fabric to the cloth headliner in the Bronco, gathering it as I went so it looked from the outside like curtains. Curtained car windows are not uncommon in New Mexico, so I hoped they would attract little notice. I attached the fabric with pins because I planned to take it down as soon as possible.

I parked the Bronco on the corner of 4th and Silver, climbed between the captain's chairs, over the folded-down back seat and into the back. I shortened the adjustable legs on the tripod, attached my refractor scope, and poked the front end between two panels of the curtains. To prevent passers-by from seeing inside, I safety-pinned the panels above and below where the scope protruded. Then I aimed the scope and adjusted the eyepiece until the image of the keypad filled the entire field on the glass.

After twenty minutes, a car pulled up to the entrance of the parking garage of Rio Grande Lofts. I watched through the scope as the driver keyed in #2330. The gate slid open, the driver drove through, and the gate closed. A second driver arrived not too long after the first. She was driving a large white SUV. The window rolled down and a red-nailed finger keyed in #9999. Once again, the gate opened, she passed through, and the gate closed.

I removed the scope from the tripod, placed it in its case and drove home.

The scope and tripod went inside with me. Breaking in to my house would be difficult, but breaking in to the Bronco would be easy even for someone like me who isn't a burglar, so I never leave anything valuable in it.

I opened the package of maple nuts and a very cold bottle of

New Mexico champagne. Yes, there is a New Mexico champagne, although it is made by a French family called Gruet. Their *Blanc de Noir* is astonishingly good. I often enjoy a few small flutes in the evening and sometimes even with breakfast.

The maple nuts and champagne made a delicious if somewhat unorthodox midnight snack, and I enjoyed it as I reflected on what I thought I had learned.

First, although I had seen only two examples, I thought it a plausible assumption that all the codes to open the entrance gate at Rio Grande Lofts were four numbers preceded by a pound sign. Second, people are not very careful when selecting codes. 9999 is easy to remember, but someone trying to gain unauthorized access would probably try all the easy codes first—1234, 1111, 9999, etc. I might be able to get in just by punching in easy-to-remember number combinations, but since I already had two codes I knew would work, I didn't plan to stand at the keypad punching and hoping.

I wanted in fast, I wanted in covertly, and I wanted out safely.

19

My first foray was intended as reconnaissance. It's not my fault that it didn't quite work out that way.

I read until one-thirty in the morning. Then I put a windbreaker over my shirt and walked downtown. I reached the garage entrance shortly after two a.m., stepped up to the keypad and punched in #2330. The gate slid open and I walked down to the parking garage of Rio Grande Lofts. It seemed almost too simple.

I ambled around the garage for a few minutes to get the lay of the concrete. There was a lot of it. Floors, pillars, walls, even the ceiling was concrete. I thought it would look better with a coat of plaster, but I guess aesthetics is not a major consideration in parking garages.

A well-lit glassed-in area illuminated the otherwise dark garage. Two elevators and a door were visible through the glass. The door to the area was locked, and another keypad was next to the knob. I stared at it for a moment and asked myself the obvious question: Why was there another keypad? Surely the same code that opened the gate wouldn't open the door. What would be the point?

But I tried it anyway. Sure enough, #2330 didn't open the door. Maybe an apartment number would do it. I tried the only apartment number I knew, 1101. Nothing happened. I tried #1101. Nothing happened.

Then I walked around the garage some more. I'm in the building, I told myself, so surely I can get past the garage. I thought back to the night I watched the keypad through my telescope, and I remembered the second entrance code I'd seen was #9999. I also remembered how people pick easy numbers. So I revisited the keypad by the door to the glassed-in area and punched in 9999. Nothing. Then I punched in #9999 and 9999#. Same result. Then I tried 1234, #1234, 1111, #1111, 2468, #2468, and 6666 just for the devil of it. Then I gave up.

You're probably smarter than I am, so you may have already realized I was going to have a problem leaving the building. If so, I can only ask where you were when I needed you?

I walked to the exit of the garage and waited for the gate to open. But of course it didn't. I tried to slide it open. I might as well have tried to slide one of the concrete columns to a different location. The sensing device was a squat pedestal covered with sheet metal, and I could see no way of removing the cover. And what would I have done had I been able to get the cover off? Cross the wires in a clever way to make the gate open? Remember this is Hubert Schuze, technophobe extraordinaire.

So I did nothing. Nothing to get out, that is. Instead, I tried the doors to all the cars. Several of them were unlocked. I guess if you park in a secure garage, you may not bother locking your car. I selected an old Mercury Grand Marquis, climbed in to the back seat, and eventually fell asleep.

The sound of a car starting woke me up at 6:40. I was cold, unshaven, hungry and needed to pee. The latter was the only one I could deal with. I waited until the newly started car departed and then drenched the right front tire of a Mercedes 700. Maybe the owner would think a dog did it.

I paced around the garage trying to warm up, running my hands through my hair, trying to stroke the creases out of my clothes and waiting for the right moment. The third person out of the elevator and through the glass door was a woman in her twenties looking poorly made up and well hung over. I patted my pockets as if I had forgotten my keys. When she pushed the door open, I grabbed it and walked in. She never looked back.

Elevator or stairs? I had the notion the elevators might stop automatically on the first floor. If the doorman saw me when the elevator opened, I'd be sunk. So I took the stairs all the way to the eleventh floor, my stomach churning from hunger and fear. My footfalls on the concrete steps sounded like gunshots and rever-berated through the hard-surfaced stairwell. I expected someone to burst through a door at any moment and demand to know who I was and what I was doing in the building. The combination of anxi-ety and climbing eleven stories had me panting like a dog by the time I reached the door to the eleventh floor, but at least I made it.

For all the good it did me. The door was locked. I may have uttered a profane epithet. Then I stood there trying to figure out why the door was locked. I guessed the door could be opened only from the hallway. That way, no one fleeing the building during a fire could accidentally enter back in if she had started out on the seventh floor, for example, miscounted in her panic, and tried to exit at the second floor thinking she had reached the safety of the ground floor.

I descended the stairs trying each doorknob in turn. They resisted my twist until I reached the first floor. I eased the door open and peered in to the lobby. A doorman was holding the front door for someone leaving the building. When he turned around, his field of vision would include the door I was holding open, so I closed it and waited.

I opened the door a few seconds later and saw the doorman's back. He was sitting on a stool staring outside. The elevator opened, and the doorman responded by turning around. I closed the door before he could see me. Then I asked myself what the devil I was doing. I answered that I had no idea.

I was cold and hungry. I wanted to go home. I suppose I could have simply walked out. The doorman might have been surprised to see a stranger depart the building, but that had to happen from time to time, didn't it? A resident could drive in to the garage with a visitor from out of town and take that person up to his apartment for the night. The next morning, the resident might go off to work and his visitor might decide to go down the block to buy a magazine. He would need to take along at least $2.95 plus sales tax.

I could walk out the front door. It might be standard procedure for the doormen to ask all visitors whose guest they were, especially if the guests expected to regain entrance after buying their magazines. What if I were asked? I could say I had enjoyed a night of unbridled passion with one of the residents who preferred to remain anonymous.

I heard footsteps in the stairway above me. One of the residents was skipping the elevator in order to get some exercise. Or maybe the elevator was too slow during the morning rush and the person was in a hurry. Of course it didn't really matter *why* the person was coming down the stairs. What mattered was that in a few seconds, I would be spotted.

So I descended to the basement. And of course the footsteps followed. I wasn't thinking fast enough. Americans don't walk to work anymore. The person coming down the stairs would be headed for his car. So when I got to the basement, I left the glassed-in area and walked between a row of parked cars. Then I bent down to tie a shoe that was not untied and saw a man come out of the stairs and walk down a different row of cars. A few moments later, I heard a car start.

Then another person emerged from the glassed-in area. I was caught in the morning rush in the basement of Rio Grande Lofts. I decided to put aside temporarily the problem of how to exit the building. I had come to reconnoiter, and I felt duty-bound to do it. I walked back to the glassed-in area, waited for the next resident to open the door, did my patting-my-pockets-for-my-keys routine and walked in the door before it closed. The man who had passed through the door turned to give me a suspicious look but decided to let it go. Maybe he was running late for work.

I strode boldly to the elevator and punched the up button, but my resolve wavered as I recalled a camera in the Albuquerque Hyatt that made me a murder suspect by placing me on a floor I had no reason to visit. A ding sounded. The little up arrow illuminated. The elevator door slid open. I craned my neck to see if I could spot a camera without it spotting me. Realizing that was stupid, I sidled in just as the door slid shut.

No camera. I suppose they were so confident in their perimeter security, they didn't worry about an intruder getting as far as the elevator. I exhaled, expecting a smooth ascent to eleven. The ride was quicker than I anticipated.

That was because it stopped at four. The doors opened to reveal a woman with impressively quaffed blond hair. She wore tan slacks, a white blouse and high heels she didn't need. She was taller than me in her bare feet.

"Going down?"

"Up," I replied and reached for the 'close door' button.

"I'll ride along," she said and stepped in before I could get the door closed. "Better to grab the elevator while you can this time of morning," she added cheerily by way of explanation.

Once she got a better look at me, she traded in cheery for wary. "Why are you going up at this time of morning?"

I gave her a wan smile and patted my pockets. "Forgot my keys."

"Looks like you forgot your iron, too," she said flatly.

She struck me as a take-charge person who would not hesitate to call security if she spotted someone suspicious in the building, and I figured I fell in that category. "Sorry," I said, "ever since my wife left me, I've been sort of disheveled. I have no idea how to iron. In fact, I think she took the iron."

It was a lame story, but I'm not good at improv.

"Why did she leave you?" she asked, unabashed.

"She met a younger man."

She seemed to relax slightly.

The elevator reached the eleventh floor and I stepped out. She stuck her foot against the door.

"Did she take your razor, too?" The woman had no shame. Then she smiled. "What's your name?"

"Hubert."

She laughed. "I'm Stella, but of course you already know that? If you need to borrow an iron, just ask. I might even show you how to use it."

Then she let the door slide shut.

As the door closed, I gave her a little wave like an idiot.

Why she thought I knew her name I couldn't say. At least our last exchange convinced me she wasn't going to alert the authorities to my presence in the building, so I went about doing what I had come there to do.

I walked up to the door of Loft 1101 and grasped the knob. I pushed it and pulled it. Then I tried to turn it. It was locked, but of course I wouldn't have opened it even had it not been. I studied the door and lock and saw everything I needed to see.

I walked the length of a hall carpeted with a low industrial loop in inoffensive beige with random squiggles of blue and green. Acoustical tiles formed the grid of the ceiling. Beige walls and green wall sconces in the shape of seashells completed the decor. If the aim was a loft look, the target had been missed.

There were eight doors with numbers on them (1101 to 1108), two elevators, and the door to the stairs. A stainless steel door eighteen inches wide and thirty inches tall was at eye level and hinged at the top. Pushing it inward revealed a shaft. I stuck my head in the shaft and saw it extended back two feet from the wall. I looked down and saw a slanted ledge three or four feet below the door. The ledge was a foot deep and covered the half of the shaft nearest the wall. Behind the ledge, the shaft continued down. I leaned in further and could see another ledge about ten feet further down.

A trash chute. I conjectured the office workers who once toiled in the building dumped their paper waste into the chute. It would fall to the basement where a custodian would shred it, burn it, bale it or whatever they did with waste paper in those days. The slanted ledges at each floor forced the dropped paper to the back of the chute so people reaching in from the floors below wouldn't be hit by the paper falling from the floors above. From the aroma, I could tell the wastepaper chute was now a garbage chute.

I pulled my head out and took a breath of fresh air. Then I stuck it back in and looked up, thinking maybe Gerstner had cleverly lodged the pots at the top of the chute. All I saw was the top of the chute.

I walked to the stairwell door and studied the lock. Then I stepped out to the stairwell, gave my Achilles tendons a workout on the stairs, went through the glassed-in area and approached the exit.

A car edged up to the exit and the gate slid open. Just after the car cleared the gate, I sprinted through. The exit ramp has a restricted view of the street, so drivers have to ease out slowly once they get past the gate. As I suspected, the driver saw me run through the gate behind her. I could have kept going. She wasn't going to apprehend me. But she might report the incident to the building's staff, and I didn't need them on high alert when I returned.

So I ran up to the driver's window and tapped on it. A pair of eyes with bright purple shadow gave me a suspicious look, which came as no surprise considering I looked like a street person. But when I made a cranking motion with my hand, she rolled down her window an inch or so.

I had my wallet in my hand. "I saw this on the ground near your car. Is it yours?"

She shook her head.

"Okay. I didn't want you to drive off without it if it was yours."

"Thank you," she said and rolled up the window.

The sun was up, the sky was clear and the air was calm. It was a pleasant walk home. I went straight to my hammock and slept until the middle of the afternoon. When I awoke, I started to prepare a very late breakfast.

20

Which I never ate. In fact, I never even cooked it because before I could get started, I heard a persistent knocking at the door to the shop and went forward to find Miss Gladys Claiborne with her dreaded chafing dish.

Sausage, onion rings, canned soup, cereal, and crackers are things most of us eat. They are ready to go and require minimum preparation. Brown the sausage, fry the onion rings, heat the soup, spread something on the cracker, pour milk over the cereal. But for the Casserole Queen, these are not foods. They are ingredients. The dish she brought contained them all. Crumbled cooked sausage was combined with corn flakes, crushed Ritz crackers, cream of corn soup, and of course the ubiquitous shredded cheddar. The onion rings were spread on the top to form a crust and the entire thing baked to into submission.

The strangest thing about these concoctions is they actually taste good. Of course sausage would probably make boiled barley taste great. I found myself asking for seconds and wondering if the same dish would be even better with chorizo substituted for the regular sausage. That's when I knew I was losing my grip. Sleeping in a parking garage will do that.

Miss G reminded me that the second Thursday of the month was coming up, and I would be welcome at the covered dish night at St. Alban's. I had gone with her once just to be nice, and now I felt bad every time I turned down the chance to return. But most of the ladies who attend are either widowed or divorced, and I felt like the prize at a raffle.

My Aunt Beatrice once dragged me to a covered dish fund-raiser at the Methodist church she attended. I believe they must have used the same recipes. Maybe they're the staples of *cuisine américaine*, and I'm ignorant because I grew up eating Consuela's Mexican cooking. I did notice at St. Alban's that Episcopalians have fancier chafing dishes than Methodists and eschew the use of paper plates and plastic forks altogether.

I also remembered that St. Alban is the patron saint of sufferers. I don't know if indigestion is a serious enough malady to rank as a suffering, but I said a small prayer to him anyway after Miss G departed. Then I took another nap to let the food settle in preparation for the cocktail hour.

21

"'A night of unbridled passion?' You were actually going to say that to the doorman?"

"It was just a phrase that came to mind. I probably would've told him it was none of his business."

"So why didn't you just walk out? Or, better still, why didn't you drive there? Then you could have driven out. And if you'd found the pots, you could have put them in the back of the Bronco. How were you going to carry them on foot anyway? Steal a pillowcase from Gerstner and sling it over your shoulder with the swagger inside?"

"I think you mean swag."

"Swag, loot, whatever you burglars call it."

"I'm not a burglar."

"Not much of one anyway."

"Look, I made no provision for carrying away the pots because I knew I wasn't going in to Gerstner's apartment."

"Loft," she corrected.

"Right. When I'm ready to actually go in, I'll want to make sure he isn't in there. I wanted to study his door so I could figure out how to get in when the time comes."

"And did you figure it out?"

"I think so, thanks to you." I told her what I had in mind and why she deserved credit for it. She suggested a different plan.

"From the way you describe it, the door doesn't sound that strong. Why don't you just take a crowbar and pry it open?"

"I don't want to damage it."

"Geez, you're breaking in to the man's house. Why the compunction about merely damaging his door?"

"I don't want him to know he's been broken in to."

"Won't he figure that out when he sees the pots are gone?"

"The pots may not be there. Maybe they're in one of those rental storage places or at his cabin in the mountains."

"He has a cabin in the mountains?"

"I have no idea. But if they're not in his apartment, I don't want him to know there was a break-in."

"Because it would put him on alert, and he might move the pots out of the cabin you don't know whether he has?"

"Right. But the first order of business is to find out whether the pots are in his apartment."

She took a sip of her drink and looked at me over the rim of the glass. "That should be easy now that you've got a girlfriend in the building."

"She's hardly a girlfriend."

"Oh, Hubie," Susannah said in a falsetto, "come by my place and I'll teach you how to iron."

"She was just being a good neighbor."

"Come on, Hubie. That's as obvious a pick-up line as I've ever heard."

"No way. She's better looking than me, taller than me and younger than me. Why would she come on to an unshaven guy in wrinkled clothes who smelled faintly of gasoline fumes?"

"Don't sell yourself short," she said and smiled. "Oops, bad choice of phrase. What I meant to say is you're a handsome guy, and the unkempt look is in these days. You should call her up. Maybe you *are* in for a night of unbridled passion in Rio Grande Lofts."

"Don't be ridiculous. Anyway, I can't call her. I don't have her number, and I can't look it up because I don't know her last name."

"Just call the building and ask for Stella."

"Hmm. What if they ask who's calling?"

"Tell them it's Hubert."

"What if they want a last name? That doorman Rawlings is very thorough."

"Make one up. She doesn't know your last name, does she?"

I felt myself perking up. "You know, Suze, you might be right. A call could get me back in the building the easy way, and even if she refuses to take the call, what have I lost?"

22

Saturday morning broke clear and crisp. At least I suppose it did. I was blissfully asleep at the time, but the day was clear and crisp when I awoke several hours after it actually broke.

A sunny October day is perfect for eating Consuela Sanchez' cooking. Of course the same could be said of a rainy day in May, a snowy day in February or a windy day in March.

I drove up the north valley to my favorite butcher where I made a large purchase and then reversed direction and drove down the south valley until I reached the unnamed dirt road to the residence of Emilio and Consuela Sanchez.

"*Bienvenido, Señor Uberto.*"

"*Buenos dias, Señor Sanchez.*"

"Consuela, she is in the garden. She is anxious to see you."

"I am anxious to see her as well, but first you can help me carry this box inside. It requires a strong man like you, Emilio."

"I am no longer strong, *amigo*. I fear the years have stolen my strength."

"Take one end of the box and we'll see."

He hoisted his end and we carried it inside.

"You see, you are still strong."

"I pray to San Vicente to keep me strong so that I may care for Consuela. What is in the box?"

"Meat."

"The box is large. Have you kept none for yourself?"

"I have no freezer. It would be a sin to let it spoil, so I bring it to you because you have room for it. And also because you know how to make *carne asada*, and perhaps I will have the chance to taste it again."

"Of that you can be sure. But come to the back and see Consuela."

She slumbered under the sun in a metal lawn chair with a blanket on her lap. Her gray hair was combed back and covered with a scarf tied under her chin. Her once plump face was drawn and ashen. She smelled faintly of antiseptic and chiles and awoke when I hugged her.

"You've been roasting *poblanos*, Señora Sanchez."

"What do I tell you, Emilio? He has the nose. But, Uberto, you must call me Consuela."

We chatted about the pecan trees they planted when they bought the lot before the house was built. We spoke of my parents, of how she had met Emilio and been relieved to see he was so handsome and of her daughter who lives in California and has not given them grandchildren even though she is nearing thirty and married. Consuela blamed it on California and expressed certainty that if Ninfa and her husband would move back to New Mexico, the children would surely come.

She didn't mention the dialysis or anything else about her health and neither did I.

She insisted on cooking lunch, and even though I knew she was not up to it, I also knew it would be impossible to dissuade her. As my nose informed me, she had roasted and peeled the *poblanos*, shredded the *quesadilla* and the *asadero* and cooked the side dish of refried beans. I watched her beat the egg whites to stiff peaks with a hand whisk, stuff the *poblanos* with the two cheeses, dip them in the egg whites and lower them into the boiling lard. She turned them deftly and removed them to a paper sack to drain.

Warm plates from the oven received *chiles rellenos* and *frijoles refritos*. Her own plate held only a small helping of the beans. Emilio opened two cans of Tecate and we dug in. Though she was obviously frail, Consuela joined in the conversation with enthusiasm and laughter, and we sat at the table for two hours.

I'm ashamed to admit I ate four *rellenos* and at least a plateful of beans. Emilio stayed with me bite for bite, with the result that when Consuela produced a large platter of *flan*, he and I groaned in unison. But of course we each ate a large rectangle of the rich custard.

I hugged Consuela and Emilio in turn. They pressed a bag of chile-roasted pecans into my hands, and we repeated our farewells several times. It was past three when I finally pulled onto the highway.

Susannah thinks I don't read enough frivolous books, so—in keeping with her running insistence that I'm a burglar—she lent me a mystery called *The Burglar who Studied Spinoza*. I chose that one because of an interest in Spinoza. Turns out there isn't much about him in the book, which is probably just as well. I'm no philosopher. I tried once to read his major work, *Ethics*. It was like running through sand, but I liked one passage that says something like, "The free man wastes no time thinking about death." I suppose Spinoza meant 'free' not as opposed to 'enslaved' but in the sense of liberated from fear.

While I was gazing at the stars in my patio, a limb from one of my cottonwoods might have fallen on my head and killed me. I don't worry about such things. Live life correctly and well each day. That's my motto. I like to think the Sanchezes share my view. They have not allowed Consuela's illness to undermine their life. They live every day according to their values and they enjoy such simple pleasures as are available to them. So being with them makes me happy, not sad.

23

My previous discussion with Susannah ended with her convincing me I had nothing to lose by calling the glamorous Stella in Rio Grande Lofts. After further consideration, I decided she was wrong.

If I got the call past the doorman and if Stella took the call, my troubles were just beginning.

"Hi, Hubert," I could hear her saying, "I'm glad you called. Why don't you pop down to the fourth floor and pick up my iron." Or worse, "Why don't I bring my iron up to eleven and show you how to use it?"

I ran through a dozen imaginary conversations with both Stella and her doorman, and I didn't like any of them. I didn't know how the phone system worked at Rio Grande Lofts. Maybe they could dial each other directly. The fact that my call was being transferred by the doorman would alert her that I was not in the building, and the first thing she would ask is where I was calling from . . . and, well, you get the picture. Calling the building didn't seem nearly so simple as Susannah and a couple of margaritas had made it sound.

So I decided to find out Stella's apartment number by watching the fourth floor and seeing which door she came from in the morning.

I had no desire to spend another night in the parking basement, so I drove the Bronco up to the keypad at 7:00 Monday morning and noticed a metal sleeve had been welded around it. You couldn't see the numbers unless you were directly in front of the keypad. My first thought was I'd been spotted spying the numbers through my telescope. When I punched in #2330 and nothing happened, I was sure of it.

I tried the other code I had seen, #9999, not thinking it would work, but it did, so I decided the changes didn't mean I had been spotted. Maybe the resident with code #2330 just decided to change his code the way people sometimes change their passwords. At least that's what my nephew Tristan tells me. I don't have any passwords.

There was a clicking sound from the direction of the gate. It drew back and I drove in.

I was dressed in business attire and carrying a brief case, so when a resident came through the door of the glassed-in area and I grabbed the door and let myself in, he didn't even look back. Maybe clothes do make the man.

I elevatored to the fourth floor, walked down the hall and opened the door to the stairwell. Once on the stairwell side of the door, I removed metal shears, wire mesh, a screwdriver and a clay plug from the briefcase. I pressed the clay into the slot where the bolt goes. I worked the metal shears around the wire mesh to create a piece the width of the metal plate around the bolt hole. Then I removed the two screws from the plate, put the mesh under it and reinserted the screws. The mesh would do triple duty—holding the clay in place, allowing it to dry and preventing the bolt from lodging in the bolt hole.

I held the door ajar and watched. A man emerged from number 409. I closed the door quietly. I heard the elevator doors open and close. Then I eased the door open again. Two other people exited their apartments and went to the elevator before Stella stepped out from number 404. She was stunning. I was preparing to move briskly up the stairs to avoid encountering her if she came towards me, but she stopped at the elevator and punched the down button.

I walked leisurely down the stairs, giving her plenty of time to exit the building. Then I opened the door, walked through the glassed-in area, got in the Bronco and drove up to the exit gate. Whatever magic it is that allows gates to distinguish cars from persons worked. It opened and I drove to my nephew's apartment.

24

Tristan is not actually my nephew. He's the grandson of my Aunt Beatrice, my mother's sister. I think that makes Tristan my second cousin once removed. Or maybe it's my first cousin twice removed. As an anthropologist, I should be an expert on kinship, but I'm not. I prefer physical anthropology—pots. Anyway, I call him my nephew and he calls me his uncle, and that's the way we feel about each other.

I stopped at Barela's Coffee House for two chorizo and egg breakfast burritos and a large black coffee. I let myself in to his apartment with my key and held the steaming coffee under his nose. When he was close enough to consciousness to groan, I shook his shoulders.

"What time is it?" he asked groggily.

"Past ten."

"At night?"

"No, the morning, and I've brought you breakfast."

"Put it on the counter and I'll eat it later." He closed his eyes.

I shook him some more. "You can't go back to sleep. The burritos will get soggy, and I need your help."

He swung his feet to the floor and stared at me. "I've got to pee." He did. Loudly with the door open.

"Didn't your mother teach you to close the door?" I yelled toward the bathroom.

"I can't hear you."

I heard a flush and then the running of the tap, so at least, I thought to myself, his hygiene is better than his manners.

He got back in bed, propped himself up on his pillow and began to eat the burritos. I wondered if I needed to reconsider my estimation of his hygiene.

"Are you going to wash the sheets when you finish breakfast?"

"Nah. I never wash them unless I have a girl coming over."

It happens quite often—girls find him irresistible. He's slightly pudgy with smooth skin and black hair that hangs down in ringlets around his neck. His large eyes have dark skin under them, so he looks like some sort of lovable animal baby. He's also a nice person, and the girls like that, too. You may wonder, in light of his love life, how we both avoid the embarrassment of my letting myself in to his apartment only to find he is not alone. The answer is we have a very sophisticated system. When he's not alone, he sticks a yellow Post-it Note on his door.

After eating both burritos, he looked in to the sack and said to the bottom of it, "Did you bring anything else?"

"Yes, a question about telephone numbers. If I have an address, is there any way to find the telephone number that goes with it?"

"There are some companies on the Internet that do that for a charge. What they've done is dump phone book data into a relational data base."

"English?"

"They have the telephone numbers in order instead of the names."

"That should work."

"Only if the person has a listed number." He stepped over to his desk and hit a few keys on his computer. I gave him Stella's address, but he came up empty.

"So there's no way to find the number?"

"Well, there is a more complete reverse directory, but only the police, firefighters, and other authorized agencies are supposed to have it."

"Oh."

He gave me a big sleepy smile. "I have one."

"I don't want you getting in trouble."

"Don't worry. Mine is an encrypted data base I got by hacking in to—"

"I don't think I want to know this. I wouldn't understand it anyway."

He entered Stella's address and gave me her telephone number.

25

The next morning, I took a clean blue shirt from my chifferobe even though I was already wearing a clean yellow one. Then I opened for business, wadded up the blue shirt, put it on the seat of the stool behind the counter, sat down on it and started reading and waiting for customers.

The reading was uninterrupted. Later that day I made a call. "Hi, Stella, this is Hubert. You remember me? We met in the—"

"Hubert! I was hoping you'd call." Her voice was lilting and her diction perfect. "Did you ever find your iron?"

"No, I really do think my wife took it."

"Why don't you come down now and I'll loan you mine and show you how to use it."

This was working as easily as Susannah predicted. I told Stella I was at work, which was true. I also told her I could be there in twenty minutes. She said she would be waiting for me. I changed into the shirt I'd been sitting on.

I realized after getting the number that I couldn't use Stella to get me in the building until after we met again. I mean, what could I say to her on the phone, "Meet me at the entrance so I can get past the doorman"?

But I figured once I got to know her, maybe we could walk in and out a few times and the doorman would see me as someone who was entitled to come and go. Maybe he would think I had moved in with her. More likely, I told myself, he would think I was her father.

And I didn't need her help at this point anyway because even though #2330 no longer worked, #9999 still did.

Or so I thought. I drove up next to the keypad and punched in #9999. Nothing happened. I tried it again thinking maybe I had mis-keyed, but nothing happened again. I sat there wondering what to do.

I remembered thinking when I first saw the codes through my telescope that there aren't that many four-digit numbers, 9999 of them to be exact. I figured the building had eighty units since there were ten floors with residences and I had seen eight numbered doors on the eleventh floor. So I did the math. The odds of hitting a live code were almost exactly 1 in 125, a lot better than the lottery. I could probably punch in one code every five seconds, twelve a minute, so the odds are I would hit a live one within 10 to 15 minutes. So I started punching codes. #0000, # 0001, #0002, . . .

And that's as far as I got because the horn interrupted me. A resident behind me wanted in. I couldn't back out because the entry is just wide enough for one vehicle, so I made the sign for confusion by throwing my hands up. The resident got out of his car and walked up to lend assistance. He was an elderly gentleman driving a Mercury Grand Marquis. I didn't tell him I had slept in his car, but I did tell him my code didn't work.

"First they changed the code for Jenkins on the second floor because someone else used it. Then they welded on this contraption, and I can hardly punch in my code now because when I bend my head down to see under the metal, my bifocals don't work."

I made sympathetic clucking sounds.

"And now they change everyone's code to five numbers. A feller would think he was living in CIA headquarters."

"It is sort of overkill," I agreed. "I not only forgot we switched to five digits, I forgot my five. I've been gone several days, and—"

"I understand. I don't drive much, so I forget the thing all the time. I have mine taped on my dashboard."

"Well, I'm sorry to trouble you, but I guess you'll just have to back out so I'll have room to—"

"Shucks, there's no reason for all that." He punched in his own code. Which I didn't have the presence of mind to catch, but so what? It was on his dashboard.

I did have the presence of mind to walk with my new neighbor to the glassed-in area and, without being too obvious about it, watched him punch in *07061. We entered the elevator and he hit seven and then turned to me. I told him four.

He was Wes, originally from Omaha, a cattle buyer who'd spent a lot of time in New Mexico and decided to move here when he retired. He was an amiable fellow whose health was failing on a number of fronts, but I exited the elevator at four in time to avoid hearing about his gall bladder operation.

The clay had dried completely and it slid easily out of the bolt hole. The stairway doors were extra strong and fireproof, and the locks that held them were industrial rather than residential, their bolt holes deep and wide. The clay piece was bulky, and I didn't have my briefcase this time, so I stuck it in my pocket. Then I went to 404 and rang the bell.

She was even more attractive than I remembered. Her makeup was so expertly applied that she seemed not to be wearing any. I knew it was makeup only because no one is born with lips that red or cheeks that rosy. Her hair was perfect. Her clothes revealed curvy hips, a small waist and full breasts.

She greeted me enthusiastically and gave me a wraparound hug. Then she started laughing. "Hubert! Is that a banana in your pocket, or are you just happy to see me?"

Oh great, I thought. She'll think I'm some sort of pervert who carries around a plastic novelty item. But she didn't look alarmed in the least.

"You're blushing."

She took my hand and led me into her apartment. "I apologize if I embarrassed you, but I've always wanted a chance to use that line, and I couldn't resist. What is that in your pocket, anyway?"

"Umm, it's just some clay. Did I tell you I'm a potter?"

"No, the only thing you told me was your wife left you and took the iron. Which is obvious because that shirt is a mess."

Both Stella and her apartment appeared to be professionally done. The dark wood floors were covered by rugs that looked hand woven by women in veils in some distant land whose name ends with 'stan'. The walls were taupe and held oil paintings of sylvan glades. The furniture was mismatched by design, a Queen Anne sofa with a wicker coffee table, a large leather club chair next to a massive ceramic vase with an elephant motif that served as an end table, a Tiffany lamp sitting on a Bombay chest.

Stella wore a white knee-length full skirt that sort of wrapped around her and a loose-fitting raw silk blouse the color of acorns. I suppose it was the casual elegance look. It was also the sexy look.

We sat on the sofa and drank tea from a silver pot on a silver tray on the wicker coffee table. When she sat her cup down, no lipstick blemished its rim. I began to think she didn't wear makeup. She had been born perfect.

She asked me about my wife, and I said it was too painful to talk about. Which was true. Making stuff up spur of the moment can be anguishing. Since I'd told her I was a potter, she asked me how pots are made, and she seemed enthralled with every detail. She was an excellent listener, and I began to relax.

We talked about this and that, and the longer we talked the shorter the distance between us became on the Queen Anne sofa. When we first sat down, King Henry VIII would have had no difficulty inserting his considerable bulk between us. But as time wore one, even the petite Anne would have been unable to do so.

She reached over and put her hand on my chest. "That shirt is a mess. Take it off, and I'll show you how to iron it."

She already had the ironing board up and the iron on. "Come over and stand close to me so you can see how this works."

I took a few tentative steps. "Closer, Hubert. Don't be shy."

I stepped closer and she made a few passes with the iron explaining how to do it. Then she handed it to me. Having been a bachelor all my life, I can wield an iron as well as the next woman, but of course I didn't want to demonstrate any skill under the circumstances, so I made a few inept movements.

"Oh, for heaven's sake," she said and took the iron back. "Stand behind me."

I did.

"Closer," she said.

I stood closer.

"Now," she said, "reach around me with your right arm and put your hand on top of mine."

She started moving the iron. I deliberately moved opposite to what I knew she would do, and that caused my body to zig when hers zagged so that we were rubbing together.

"Are you flirting with me, or are you really that bad at ironing?" she asked lightheartedly.

"It's awkward because I'm left handed."

"Well I can't iron left-handed, so I'll just have to steady you. Put your left hand on the iron."

I did.

"Give me your right hand."

I did and she pulled it forward and placed it on her stomach so that I was now virtually embracing her from behind.

"Now you can get a feel for it," she said, and by then I was definitely getting a feel for it. By the time she finished, the clay wasn't the only thing that . . . well, no need to get graphic.

After she released me, she turned around and held up my shirt. "See, not a wrinkle to be seen. Of course you ironed this one with the instructor in the cockpit, didn't you? It's time for you to solo. You didn't happen to bring another wrinkled shirt, did you?"

I admitted I hadn't. Somehow I was confident she knew that.

"Would you mind practicing on mine?"

I uttered a squeaky "no" and had a flashback to age fourteen when my voice changed.

She slowly removed her blouse and held it in her right hand at arm's length away from her body, bending her left arm over her breasts in a halfhearted attempt to hide the fact that she was wearing nothing under the shirt.

I was trying to remain composed. "You are astonishingly beautiful," I told her, "but we really don't know each other very well, and—"

"Are you turning me down, Hubert?"

She dropped the shirt and her left arm. My pulse revved up still further. "No, it's just that—"

She stepped up and put her arms around me. "I know. You're married. But she left you. For a younger man. So why deny yourself?" Then she kissed me and slid her hands into my clothes and her tongue into my mouth, and all resistance melted away.

What can I tell you? It was great. Maybe because it had been a long drought for me, but I think it was mainly because Stella had an incredible body and was quite eager to put it through its paces. You may recall me saying earlier that I was seduced in the elevator. Not technically correct, but that's where it started. You may also remember my quip that digging up pots might be better than sex.

It isn't.

My romp with Stella is sort of the story of my life. Or at least my love life. I can craft a pot like an Anasazi from a thousand years ago. I can dig for ancient artifacts by the light of the moon. I can cook enchiladas to die for. I can solve quadratic equations. But when I try to ask a woman for a date, my talents disappear, my I.Q. drops forty points and I perspire like a swine in a sweat lodge.

There is, however, an upside to this malady. Some women—for reasons known only to God or perhaps to Charles Darwin—find ineptitude irresistible in a man. To be vulnerable is to be lovable. 'Tis untrue that faint heart ne'er won fair maiden. This peculiar adaptation of *Homo sapiens*—this desire of some women to embrace the bashful—is what prevents me from the chaste life of a monk.

Mind you, this is not a complaint.

26

"That is so romantic. And sexy, too. Sort of like strip ironing instead of strip poker. But why are you here? You should be in Rio Grande Lofts enjoying that night of unbridled passion you were going to mention to the doorman."

I told Susannah what happened, but in no more detail than I told you. She and I are best friends, but some things are too personal to share with anyone.

"She had to go to work," I explained.

"At three in the afternoon? What does she do?"

"I have no idea."

"Does she know what you do?"

"I didn't tell her I'm a burglar, if that's what you mean."

"No, I mean does she know you're a potter?"

"Uh, yeah, she does in fact." I told Susannah about the piece of clay.

"That's the funniest thing I've ever heard. You're blushing."

I seemed to be doing a lot of that lately. "With good reason."

"So you didn't ask what sort of work she does?"

"No, she seemed interested in pot making, so we talked a lot about that, and then after . . . well, she said she had to get to work and for me to give her a call. But now I remember she did say something sort of odd. She asked me not to call her at work."

"That's not odd. A lot of work places don't let employees take personal . . . oh, I see what you mean. Since she hasn't told you where she works, how could you call her there anyway?"

"Exactly. She thought I knew her when we first met. Maybe she also thinks I know where she works."

"Maybe you do."

"Know her or know where she works?"

"Both."

"Hmm. Maybe so. I didn't think I recognized her when I first saw her, but she seems more familiar now."

"Well, I would think so, Hubert. I would say you two are both quite familiar to each other now."

"No, I mean I think I may have seen her before. Maybe she's a waitress."

"Restaurants don't have shifts that begin at three, and waitresses don't earn enough money to live in Rio Grande Lofts and hire professional decorators."

"Oh. Well, I've got a bigger problem than trying to remember if I know her somehow."

"What's that?"

"My plan was to get to know her, maybe have coffee a couple of times, go to lunch, and then see if I could somehow gain unrestricted access to the building. I never imagined we would . . . you know, the first time I went to her place. And it wasn't even a date. She was just going to show me how to iron, for heaven's sake."

"Well, I'd say she accomplished that, Hubert. She heated you up, flattened you out, and took away all your wrinkles."

"Oh, stop it," I said, but I couldn't help laughing.

"Are you telling me you're disappointed things went faster than your go-slow plan?"

"Yes, I am. I admit it was great, but I did try to resist. I was taken by surprise. Now she'll be expecting me to drop down and see her or vice versa."

"What's vice versa here, see her and drop down?"

I blushed again. "No, she may want to come up to my loft on the eleventh floor."

"And you don't have a loft on the eleventh floor."

"Or any other floor, and now she'll find that out for sure."

27

Tristan's door had a yellow Post-it Note the next morning. He studies computer science and has two sources of income. He does odd jobs I don't understand like setting up websites, writing macros and installing software. And he accepts what he describes as loans from me.

He also has a volunteer job trying to bring me in to the digital age. I've probably read over 10,000 books while waiting for customers, so I have more information than most people. Susannah says most of it is useless. But the digital age is not about information. And it's certainly not about age. Most everyone in it is under thirty. Neither does it—etymology not withstanding—have anything to do with your fingers. The digital age is about gadgets.

I may be the only person on the planet who doesn't own a cell phone. Tristan has, however, introduced me to a few other electronic widgets. My favorite is satellite radio because I can listen to Trummy Young, Ella Fitzgerald, Duke Ellington, Lionel Hampton, Jack Teagarden and all my favorites at any time. My second gadget is a laser beam across the door of my shop that triggers a bong sound when anyone enters or leaves. I didn't really want it because I already had a little bell dangling on an arm above the door that served the same purpose with a more pleasurable sound, but Tristan wanted to do it, and I gave in.

I thought technology would intrude no further than the radio and laser, but then the three goons came in to my shop with their baseball bats. We live in an unruly world, and I decided I might as well face facts and secure my stores. Which is why I had come to see Tristan again. That and the fact that I have great affection for him.

Tristan dwells a block south of Central near the University and a block east of a coffee shop that's a popular hangout of the students. I wrote the name of the coffee shop on the yellow Post-It Note and went to the coffee shop to have breakfast.

Which I didn't because there was nothing fit to eat on the menu. There was nothing fit to eat on a plate for that matter, so I had coffee and amused myself by observing the tattoos and body piercings sported by the students. It was a little like being an anthropologist in New Guinea. I only imagined that. I've never been to New Guinea. In fact, I've never been outside the U.S. except once when I walked across the Rio Grande from El Paso to Juarez, Mexico.

My conclusion as a professional anthropologist is that American society is currently stratified along an age line of about forty. The only people above that line who have tattoos are former sailors who got too drunk in Manila and woke up the next morning with something they have since come to regret. I speak here of tattoos. The other thing some of them woke up with can be cured with penicillin. The only people above the stratification line who have metal in their bodies are those who've had a hip or knee replacement.

Below this dividing line, many have metal stuck in their noses, cheeks, tongues and God knows where else. The older people think the younger ones will be unable to enter professions such as law because lawyers don't have tattoos or piercings.

But the situation is temporary. The obvious fact being overlooked is that all the current lawyers will die, not an altogether bad thing. The only replacements will be from among the current crop of young people with their body adornments. So the stratification will disappear until some future generation decides it's cool *not* to decorate themselves as their elders have done, and we will then have the same stratification, but in reverse.

I was wondering whether my profound conclusion deserved to be added to my Schuze's Anthropological Premises (SAPs) when Tristan arrived. He was wearing black cotton pants with a drawstring and a Sierra Club sweatshirt. If he has any tattoos or piercings, they are located in areas not visible in public. What he does have is a layer of baby fat he hasn't yet outgrown and what all the girls seem to think of as bedroom eyes.

"I hope you didn't leave your friend on my account."

"Actually, Uncle Hubert, I was glad to have an excuse to get away."

"It didn't go well?"

"You might say it went too well. She asked me if she could leave a few things at my apartment."

"Like clothes and a toothbrush?"

"Something like that."

"And what did you say?"

"I said I'd have to check with you."

"Why me?"

"Well, you are sort of a surrogate parent."

"I'm honored you think so, Tristan, but you don't normally consult me on such things."

"Yeah, well I didn't really want to consult you. I was just buying time."

"You haven't made any promises to the young lady, have you?"

"No! In fact, she invited herself over last night. We've had a few dates, and she's fun to be with, but she's sort of pushy."

I thought about Stella. "Pushy is not always bad."

"Really? I guess I hadn't thought about that. It makes me uncomfortable though. Will you buy me a coffee?"

"Sure."

He smiled. "How about breakfast?"

"Sure."

He ordered a cappuccino and something called the Lobo Special, hash browns smothered with chili and cheese. That's chili as in ground beef, beans, tomato sauce, and chile powder, not chile as in the only green vegetable that actually tastes good.

"Maybe I will consult you," he said between bites.

"Okay, here's my advice. Tell her I pay the rent for the apartment, and I don't allow anyone to reside there except you."

"Yes sir," he said cheerily between bites. And those were the last bites because the entire breakfast had disappeared.

I told him about the pot smashing and my desire to protect my shops. He suggested a magnetic lock that would release only when I pushed a button under the counter. The doors to both shops have windows in them, so I could screen people before letting them in. I didn't much like the idea, but I told him to install the locks.

I asked him how he was doing and he said he was broke, so I slipped him a hundred dollars.

"Thanks. Now I can pay for my own breakfast."

I paid anyway.

28

After my visit with Tristan, I fabricated nine duplicates of the clay piece I had retrieved from the fourth floor stairwell bolt hole.

I thought about making an extra one for Stella as a gag gift, but then I came to my senses.

I opened the store and settled behind the counter with the book on Ptolemy. It's the sort of reading Susannah gives me a hard time about because nothing I learn from it will have any practical application.

As I was thinking about Susannah, I looked up and there she was, coming down the street with a coffee in each hand. She walked methodically up to my door and kicked on it.

I drew back the door and asked, "To what do I owe the honor of—"

"Close the shop, Hubie, and let's sit down in your kitchen."

I had just opened, but what difference did it make? The odds were I wouldn't have any customers, so I did as I was told and followed her back. "You brought me—"

"Do you have any Kahlua?"

"Yes, but it's—"

"Get it. And two mugs."

She took the tops off the paper cups and poured the contents into the mugs. I handed her the Kahlua and she poured a generous shot in to one of my mugs.

"You want some?"

I shook my head and she took a large gulp of her liquor-laced coffee.

She appeared shell-shocked. She looked up like she was going to say something and then she swallowed another gulp of the coffee. She stared down at her cup and took several deep breaths. "I know you're not the type to say I told you so, but you can say it if you want to."

"Why would I want—"

"I just had my first computer-dating experience."

"Oh."

"The guy's message to me was witty and urbane. He poked fun at computer dating and even admitted he hadn't told anyone he was doing it because he thought it was hokey. Then he wrote—here, let me read it to you," she said and pulled a crumpled paper from her purse. "He wrote, 'I tried the singles bars, but all the gaiety seemed so forced, all the patrons so young. I sat at the bar and wondered what cruel twist of fate had placed me in this farce. So I figured computer dating couldn't be any worse. After the first hundred messages I got, I decided I was wrong. It was worse. Then I read what you said, and I thought I sensed a kindred spirit.' Doesn't that sound great? Isn't that exactly the sort of response I was hoping for when I placed that edgy paragraph you suggested?"

"Actually," I corrected, "I didn't suggest—"

"He writes well, doesn't he?"

I thought 'cruel twist of fate' was hackneyed but didn't say so.

"Maybe I should have suspected? He writes well. He thinks the people in singles bars are too young, and his name is Frederick. That's not all that common a name. Maybe I subconsciously didn't want anything to go wrong, so I suppressed my caution."

"Susannah?"

"Yes?"

"I have no idea what you're talking about."

"I arranged to meet the guy who wrote what I just read to you. In fact, I met him a few minutes ago at Barela's Coffee House." She took another slug of coffee.

"And?" I prompted.

"And I recognized him."

I paused briefly to think. "Well, of course you recognized him. That's sort of the point, isn't it? What did he do? Wear a monocle? Hold a rose between his teeth?"

"I knew him. I mean he was someone I already knew."

"Why would you need a computer dating service to arrange a meeting with someone you already knew?"

"Geez, Hubert, you are hopeless. Do you have any ice?"

I took a tray from the fridge and dropped a couple of cubes in her empty mug. She poured some Kahlua over the ice.

"You want some more coffee? I could brew some."

"No thanks, straight Kahlua is fine. You don't give your last name in computer dating. That's supposed to keep freaks from finding out where you live."

"So you do have to do something like wear a monocle," I said triumphantly.

She rolled her eyes to indicate my example was ridiculous, but she said I was right. "He said he had a thin moustache and would be wearing a black windbreaker. I said I would have on a green corduroy dress. So I walked in, glanced around and spotted a man with a thin moustache and a black windbreaker, and it was him."

"Of course it was him. How many people wear thin mustaches and black windbreakers? And on top of that, he was there at the right time and—"

"No. Not him as in the person I was supposed to look for. *Him*—the person I already know."

Now I was really confused.

"See if you can guess who it was."

"Which one? The him you were supposed to look for or the him you already know?"

"It's one person."

"Oh."

"Let me give you the clues again. Well-educated, old enough to think people in singles bars are too young, has a thin moustache and is named Frederick."

"Well, I'm relatively well-educated and I think people in singles bars are too young, but I'm not named Frederick, and I've always been clean-shaven, so it wasn't me."

"Come on, be serious. I really want to know if you can guess this."

"Okay, was it Frederick March?"

"Who the hell is Frederick March?"

"He's a famous actor, well-educated, often sports a thin moustache and has the right name. I wouldn't be surprised if he wears a black windbreaker. He's quite dashing."

"Do I know any famous actors?"

"I suppose not. Anyway, now that I think about it, Frederick March is probably dead."

"Geez. One more clue. He works at the University."

I mulled it over. "Frederick. Thin moustache. Since you keep mentioning education, I assume he's a faculty member. I can't think of . . . oh, no. It wasn't—"

"Frederick Blass? Yes it was."

"The head of the art department?"

"The very one."

"What did you do?"

"I turned away to leave, but he had already spotted me."

"How do you know that?"

"Because he called my name. And then when I turned to face him, he said—God, this is so embarrassing—'Am I so unattractive that you would flee without saying hello?'"

"Why didn't you just keep walking when he called your name? He couldn't be sure you were the one he was waiting for."

"Of course he was sure. How many people wear green corduroy dresses? God, I'm so stupid. I picked that dress because it's so easy to spot. What I should have done is said I'd be the one in the white blouse. That way I could have made a clean getaway. Well, I've learned something for the next time."

I couldn't believe she was contemplating a next time, but this didn't seem like a good time to argue the point. "Meanwhile, what are you going to do about this time?"

"Well, he invited me to a party."

"You didn't accept, did you?"

"I did."

"Susannah! You can't go out with your department head."

"He's not my department head. You're making the mistake everyone makes. Art history and studio art are not in the same department. In fact, they aren't even in the same college. Studio art is in the college of fine arts, and art history is in the college of humanities."

"That sounds like a Clintonesque quibble to me. You're a student and he's a faculty member, and . . . and . . ." And I didn't know what. I found the whole idea disturbing, but I couldn't articulate why.

"I'm not one of his students. He has no say in my academic progress. And on top of that, he is rather handsome."

"He's old enough to be your father," I said and then immediately wished I hadn't.

"I'd guess he's around forty, and I'm almost thirty. That's not such a big deal."

"I guess not."

Susannah seemed to relax for the first time since she crossed my threshold. "There's another reason I agreed to go to the party."

I really didn't want to talk about it anymore.

"Don't you want to know what that reason is?"

"Not really."

"Come on, don't be a fuddy-duddy. I promise you'll like this reason."

"Just tell me it's not because he has a thin moustache."

"No. It's because the party is at his apartment."

"Why would I like that?"

"Because he lives in Rio Grande Lofts."

29

The real coincidence was not that Ognan Gerstner and Frederick Blass both lived in Rio Grande Lofts. Many of the residents are university people who came here from back East where high-rise living is common. We Westerners like our space. I doubt there's a single native New Mexican living in Rio Grande Lofts.

The real coincidence was that I wanted in and was invited. Why would Blass let his date bring a date? Well, it turns out Susannah and Blass didn't have a date exactly. She and he had chatted after the rocky start, and she told him the reason she tried to dodge the meeting was not his looks—she actually told him he was attractive! But she felt uncomfortable when she saw who he was.

He was very understanding, of course, and told her the thing he liked least about computer dating was the sense of being pushed into a relationship, the idea that the very fact of signing up almost committed you to pursuing a relationship, and wouldn't it be better if they just let things flow now that they knew each other. And by the way, he added, he was glad they did now know each other. Very slick. Probably said something hackneyed about 'respecting her space'. I mean, anyone who would write *cruel twist of fate*.

So Susannah wasn't really bringing a date to the party. She had asked him if she could bring a friend, and he graciously agreed. Of course if he found out I planned to break in to his neighbor's apartment, the invitation would likely be withdrawn.

I didn't plan for him or anyone else to find out. And to that end, I had to have the run of the place once I got in. I needed to go back before the party to finish my clay plug project and see if my plan for opening Gerstner's door would work.

I drove to Rio Grande Lofts after Susannah left, punched in #07114, and watched in satisfaction as the gate slid open. Where did I get that code? I read it off the dashboard of the Mercury Grand Marquis after my romp with Stella.

I parked the Bronco and walked to the glassed-in area where I punched in the other code I had picked up from Wes. I rode the elevator to two, transited the hallway from elevator door to stairway door, and stuck a clay plug in the bolt hole. Then I repeated the process on each floor, ending up on eleven.

Where I knocked loudly on Gerstner's door. What was I planning to do if he opened it? Nothing. I had run back to the stairwell and was standing inside it with my ear against the door. No sound came from the hall.

I returned to Gerstner's door and put my ear to it. Silence. I extracted from my pocket a handful of plastic chips the size of playing cards, samples from an artists supply store. They came in various colors, which I understood, and various thicknesses which I didn't because they were measured in mils. I have no idea what a mil is. It's very thin, though.

The first time I had grasped Gerstner's door after spending the night in the parking garage, I noticed it had a certain amount of give like all normal doors, and the gap between the door and the jamb was also normal, perhaps a quarter of an inch. I don't know how many mils that is.

It was a perfectly normal door and it fit well enough for any purpose short of maintaining a watertight seal. Or preventing someone from loiding it. That's a word I learned from the book Susannah gave me about the burglar who studied Spinoza. It means to force a spring-loaded lock bolt out of its jamb by prying it with a piece of celluloid. The loid has to be flexible enough to slip between the door and the jamb and then bend around the bolt, and it has to be firm enough to force the bolt out as it bends. That's why I had a variety.

I figured plastic would work as well as celluloid. The burglar book says you can also do it with a credit card, but despite the best efforts of the banking industry who are constantly pre-qualifying me, I keep only one credit card, and I didn't want to risk its destruction.

You know those letters from the banks? They even tell you you're pre-qualified on the outside of the envelope. It's is a peculiar term, isn't it? It actually means qualified, as in they will give you the card. It's like pre-boarding a plane. When you are allowed to pre-board, you actually get on the plane. So it's not pre-boarding, it's boarding. Oh well. Every specialty has its own jargon, and I suppose advertising lingo isn't any worse than anthropology-speak.

I tried the thinnest piece of plastic first. It slid in easily, but no matter how hard I pressed, nothing happened. I tried the stiffest piece second but it wouldn't bend around the bolt. The third piece was perfect, thin enough to snake around the bolt, thick enough to force it back.

The protagonist in the burglar book Susannah gave me is named Bernie Rhodenbarr. When he first steps into a house he intends to burgle, he experiences the thrill of having picked the lock and a rush from being where he shouldn't be. He loves to walk around the place and get a feel for it, sit in an easy chair, sip some of the owner's cognac and imagine what it would be like to live in the apartment he is burgling. *Sang-froid* is his middle name.

My middle name must be *sang-nerveux*. I guess that's the difference between fiction and real life. When you break in to a house in real life, the one thing uppermost in your mind—the *idée fixe* you cannot shake—is that someone is going to walk in on you. And of course that's exactly what happened.

But not before searched the place. And not before I saw the pot. The first thing to do, I had already decided, was to make absolutely sure no one was there. My knock might not have roused a heavy sleeper. I crept silently from the living room to the kitchen, then to the dining area, into a short hall, a bedroom, back to the hall, into a hall bathroom, to the hall again, into a second larger bedroom and finally into another bath off the larger bedroom. Unless someone was hiding in a closet, I was the only person there.

Searching the place turned out to be easier than I had expected. Since I was in the master bedroom, I started there. The only places large enough for a pot were the cabinet under the lavatory, the closet and under the bed. The cabinet held a spare roll of toilet paper, some cleaning supplies and a few toiletries. The closet contained one pair of men's shoes, one shoe without a mate, three pairs of pants, a jacket, several shirts and a baseball cap. There was nothing under the bed except some scary-looking dust bunnies.

The first bedroom had been empty, but I went back and checked the closet to be sure. It was also empty. A hall closet held a vacuum cleaner, a few linens and towels, an unopened box of tissues, a can of paint and a partial roll of wallpaper.

I walked back to the living area. Nothing on the walls. Nothing on the end table or the coffee table or the Parsons table behind the couch. Nothing under the couch and nothing hidden in the cushions. There was some change under them. I left it there.

The kitchen had the usual array of cabinets and appliances. There were no pots in the dishwasher, the oven or the refrigerator. There were a few pots in the cabinets but all of the metal variety. There were some dishes and a few cans and boxes of various food items. There was an electric can opener on the counter. I pushed the lever down for no reason and nothing happened. It was broken.

The dining area had a cheap laminate table and matching hutch with shelves, two drawers and two doors. The shelves were empty. One of the drawers held some placemats and napkins. The other one was stuffed full of papers. The pot was behind the left door.

I held it in my hand and got that feeling I get when I dig up ancient pots. It was a magnificent piece. Looking at it was like gazing at the stars. I felt insignificant as an individual but also somehow at peace as part of a universe that contained such an awesome object. I wished I could meet the potter and watch her work.

It was one of the Ma pots. I was sure about that. But there was something odd about the design, and I felt as I looked at it that I suddenly had everything I needed to figure out exactly what was going on. And at the same time, I thought I understood even less than I had before.

I should have left right then, but I started thinking about why the place was so sparsely kitted out. I stood there while the idea incubated in my mind. I heard a click. It was not the light bulb going on over my head. It was a key turning in the lock.

I replaced the pot and ducked under the Parsons table behind the sofa. I listened to footsteps across the carpet. They stopped. I peered under the sofa and saw a shiny pair of what I think are called Mary Janes, except there were tassels where the strap would normally be. Or maybe it was a strap with tassels. Despite my name, I don't know much about shoes.

The intruder . . . wait, *I* was the intruder. Okay, the person in the patent leather shoes must have been deciding where to go, because after a few seconds she started towards the dining area, which was a bad decision from my vantage point because as soon as she cleared the couch, I would be visible from her vantage point.

I was debating whether to make a dash for the front door as soon as she came past the sofa, but before the debate reached a conclusion, she veered to the hall. Then the sound of her footfalls changed as she moved onto a hard surface. She was on the tiles in the hall bathroom. I heard the clack of a toilet seat being lowered.

I slipped out the front door and walked down to the basement. I cracked the door and ascertained no one was in the glassed in area. I went through it quickly and scooted over to the Bronco. I locked myself inside and scrunched down to where I could barely see over the steering wheel.

I stayed that way for an hour. Several women passed through the basement, none wearing the shoes I had seen. I abandoned my surveillance and left.

30

Making pottery is like making bread. Start with good ingredients, do a lot of kneading, select the shape you want and bake. I still wonder why I couldn't make decent bread.

I got through the first two steps, but when I started on the shape I intended to copy—a shallow bowl by Joseph Latoma from San Felipe—I couldn't get it. I pushed and prodded and started over several times without making any progress. I hadn't had my hands in clay for several weeks, so I put it down to being rusty.

The next thing I knew, the bells of San Felipe De Neri were telling me it was noon. I had been working fruitlessly for two hours. I decided to give up and get some fresh air. I walked over to the church and sat on the adobe banquette next to the gate in the warm noon sun. Then I fell asleep. Maybe it was the warm sun. Or maybe it was the champagne and chorizo I had for breakfast.

I awoke under a shadow and looked up to see Father Groaz. He's a bear of a man, over six feet tall with a barrel chest, bushy beard and shiny black eyes. His collar is always clean and starched, but the rest of his clothes usually look like he slept in them. Since he had just finished mass, he was in his robe, and he looked like Rasputin's friendly uncle.

"Good Morning, Hubert," he said. Except it sounded like "Gud marnik, Youbird." He talks like an Eastern Bloc spy in a B movie from the fifties, but at least he speaks so slowly that you have time to unravel the accent.

I sat up straight and wished him the same.

"You missed mass again."

"I'm not Catholic, Father."

"Wall," he drawled, "We dahnt check I.D.s at the door."

"That's good to know. How's your Spanish, Father?"

"Thot's a vahry nice way to say my Anglish iz poor," he laughed, "baht my Spanish iz batter, and as you know, my Latin iz pearfeck."

"It's a very conservative parish. I suspect they would prefer you to give the litany in Latin."

He gave me a conspiratorial smile. "Come to Mass and discover if I do."

"So how did you happen to be assigned here?"

He shrugged. "Pearhaps woss becoss I was near. I woss in Jemez."

I noticed his pronunciation of Jemez was perfect. There's a retreat for wayward priests up there.

"I assume you were on the staff?"

He laughed roundly. "You thank mebbe I woss inmate?"

We chatted a while longer until I saw my nephew's jalopy headed towards my shop. I took my leave and found Tristan at my front door with a box of gadgets.

After I let him in, he said, "It smells like Barela's in here."

"What you smell is chorizo. Want some?"

"Too greasy for me."

He laughed his rumbling laugh and put the box on my counter. "What we have here is a laser for the door to your new shop to alert you to someone coming in. You know how it works because you already have one on the door to the old shop."

I never had understood how it worked, but I nodded anyway.

"And here we have two electromagnetic door locks operated by pushbuttons I can install under your counters. Or, if you want something really cool, I can set it up to be operated by a remote. I know you don't have a television, but you do know what a remote is, don't you?"

"Yes, I know what a remote is. It sends something like a radio signal to the television to turn it on and change channels."

"That's right." He has the smile of a ten-year-old with a shiny bike on Christmas morning. He seemed genuinely pleased that I knew how a remote worked.

"What I don't understand is how a remote can operate an electric lock."

"Electromagnetic."

"Whatever. If the lock uses electricity, how can a remote operate it? A remote can't send electrical current through the air, can it?"

"That's funny, Uncle Hubert. No, a remote sends radio waves like you said. An electromagnetic lock is activated by turning it off. Isn't that cool? Toasters and TVs and things do what you want them to do when you turn them on. But an electromagnetic lock opens when you turn it *off*. The magnet holds the door shut. But it's not a natural magnet like a lodestone. It's a winding that magnetizes only when current runs through it. So if you interrupt the current, the door unlocks. All the remote has to do is send a signal to a solenoid that—"

"I don't need the explanation, just the installation."

He smiled and set to work.

31

"Is that what you're wearing to the party?"

I had on grey trousers, a white oxford cloth shirt open at the collar, and a navy blazer. I looked down at my clothes. "Is this inappropriate?"

"No, but it's sort of . . . ordinary. I think the people Blass invites tend towards flamboyance."

"I'm not a flamboyant guy, Suze."

"I know that. Maybe you could wear an ascot tonight?"

"I don't own an ascot."

"Hmm. How about a print shirt?"

"All my shirts are solid colors."

"How about one that's not button-down? Even better, how about one of those shirts where the collar is a different color from the body?"

"Suze, I'm not worried about what I'm going to wear, okay? I'm worried that Ognan Gerstner might be there."

"I wouldn't worry about that. Blass told me it's mostly arty people."

"Yeah, but they were fellow department heads before Gerstner retired, and they live in the same building."

"They were department heads in different colleges. They reported to different deans, attended different meetings, and worked in separate buildings. Besides, you told me Gerstner was a stick-in-the-mud. The parties Blass throws are famous for their guest lists: big-name artists, rich collectors, politicians, people with—"

"Flamboyant clothes."

"Exactly."

"Well, I hope you're right. Having Ognan there could be awkward."

A sneaky smile slid onto her face. "It might be a blessing. You could burgle his apartment while being absolutely certain he wasn't in it."

"Hmm."

"What kind of name is Ognan?"

"It's Slavic."

"But isn't Gerstner a German name?"

"Originally maybe, but it's not unusual for a Czech to have a German name."

"What sort of name is Schuze?"

"It's pedestrian."

"Very funny. Seriously, what is it?"

"It's American."

"Yeah, that's what I thought about my own name growing up. Then some kid in the first grade asked me about my name as if it were strange."

"Well, Inchaustigui isn't exactly a garden variety name."

"But I didn't know that, did I? I mean, all my family had that name, so to me it was as ordinary as Smith or Sanchez."

"So what did you tell the kid?'

"Same as you. I said my name was American. But when I got home from school, I asked my mother and she said it was Basque. It was a weird feeling. On the one hand I felt special because I was Basque, although I had no idea what that meant. But on the other hand, I was worried I wasn't normal because none of the other kids in school were Basque."

"Well, Susannah, I think you were right on both counts. You are not normal and you are definitely special."

"I'll take that as a compliment."

"Is that what you're wearing to the party?"

"Don't be ridiculous. I'm wearing something special, which you'll see when you pick me up."

Susannah went home to get ready, and I went to Old Town T-Shirts and Candle Power and bought an outrageous yellow silk ascot with a repeating pattern of red Zia suns. You may know the symbol from the State Flag of New Mexico.

32

We arrived fashionably late and—wouldn't you know it—Rawlings was on duty, looking like an obedient mastiff.

"Susannah Inchaustigui for Frederick Blass," she told him.

He looked at me with an expression both solicitous and suspicious. "And you, sir?"

"Mr. Inchaustigui," I said. Susannah shot me a look but said nothing. Rawlings picked up the phone and punched in some numbers.

"Susannah Inchaustigui and her *father*, sir." I think the italics were for me rather than Blass. He hung up and said, "Have a pleasant evening," but I don't think he meant it.

"Mr. Inchaustigui?" Susannah said once we were in the elevator and the doors had closed.

"I didn't want to give him my name," I said sheepishly.

"So you gave him mine?"

"He already had yours."

We exited the elevator at ten and as Susannah punched the doorbell at 1009, I jerked the ascot off and stuck it in a pocket. The person who answered was not Frederick Blass. I knew this immediately from the fact that she had no moustache. What she did have was an ivory complexion with knobby cheekbones and a bulbous nose. Her face looked like a ski run with moguls. She was a stout creature with lank brown hair and a crooked smile. "Hello, whoever you are. Freddie is pouring drinks, so I'm playing door-person." The 'so' came out as 'show'.

She used her own drink to point towards Freddie and sloshed a bit of it on a Persian carpet that looked to my untrained eye like it had been woven when that country was still called Persia.

"I'm Bertha," she said. "Bertha Twins," she added and laughed. Then she hiccupped. "Actually, I'm Bertha Zell. And you two are much too attractive to be associating with this crowd. But come in anyway."

I peered around Bertha to see if I recognized anyone. I didn't, but the place was crowded.

"I'm Susannah Inchaustigui, and this is Hubert Schuze."

"I'm sure you are," said Bertha. 'Sure' came out as 'sur'. "Freddie is getting drinks for the others—but I already said that, I think. Let me guess what you'll be drinking." She leaned back and studied us with a cocked eye. "Champagne I should think."

"That's exactly what we want," I said. "How did you guess?"

"You're an awful liar. I think I'm going to like you."

She went to get our drinks and a man to my right said, "Pay her no mind. She's drunk."

"But charming."

"No, not charming, just drunk."

I shrugged.

"I didn't get your name," he said.

"That's because I didn't give it to you."

"You're not charming either."

"I am when I want to be."

Susannah was tugging at my sleeve. "Come on, Hubie, let's go say hello to our host."

The fellow next to me grabbed my arm. "I know you."

"I don't think so," I responded, and started to leave, but Bertha showed up with our champagne in elegant flutes.

"I see you've met Horace, our official curmudgeon. Horace Arthur, this is Ms. Susannah Inchaustigui and Mr. Hubert Schuze." She turned to me with a broad smile. "You're surprised a drunk could remember two such unusual names, are you not?"

"I are not," I said. "Nothing you could do would surprise me."

"But who I did it with might," she said and laughed roundly.

"You are not charming," Horace said to her, "and neither are you funny."

Bertha said, "See if you can do anything with him, Hubert. I certainly can't." She took Susannah's arm and walked away.

"You seem to be stuck with me," Horace said.

His Mexican wedding shirt topped khakis and Birkenstocks. He was a couple of inches taller than me but his slouch put his eyes at the level of mine. Mine are an intriguing shade of brown. His were the color of caked mustard and surrounded by glasses with turquoise-colored frames.

"Hubert Schuze!" he cried out too loudly. "Of course! I knew I recognized your name. You're the pot thief."

"Pot *merchant*," I corrected.

"Thief, merchant. It comes to the same thing, doesn't it?"

"I don't think so."

"Well, it does. Of course a thief steals from you directly. A merchant's just the middleman. But you both profit from someone else's labor."

I smiled disarmingly. "Are you always so disagreeable?"

"He is," said Frederick Blass who had walked up without me noticing. "He is also frequently tenebrous, but he is seldom boring."

"Freddie uses words like 'tenebrous' only around English faculty," Horace said flatly. "Around the art faculty he merely grunts."

Blass turned to me. "I overheard what Horace said. So you're Hubert Schuze. It's grand to meet you."

"Don't fawn, Freddie. He's a pot thief."

"Exactly. That makes him an art hero in my book." He waved a hand expansively. "Should all the museums of the world return their Matisses to France? Send back their Vermeers to Holland? Of course not. Look around this room. If I had to repatriate everything you see to the ethnic group it came from, we'd be sitting on bare floors." He glanced at my drink. "And we'd be drinking water in plastic. The champagne is from France and the flute from Poland."

"Maybe Schuze could play Chopin on it," said Horace.

Freddie and I both ignored him.

I was tempted to tell Freddie the champagne was inferior to New Mexico's Gruet but resisted.

I could see why his guests, Horace excluded, dressed flamboyantly. They needed to keep up with Freddie. He wore a blousy powder blue shirt made of a shiny fabric like silk or satin with concealed buttons and drawstring wrists. Under the loose-fitting shirt was a pair of tight-fitting black slacks and high heel ankle boots with silver toe plates. I half expected him to break into a *flamenco*.

His place looked like the main hall in a major gallery. Blass owned two units and had removed the wall between them and all the partitions in the second unit. He even removed the second kitchen in order to have a large space to entertain and display.

Unlike Gerstner's and Stella's units, this one looked like a loft. The suspended ceiling had been removed and the ducts and wires painted black and left exposed. Industrial track lighting illuminated the paintings and sculptures.

In addition to the Persian carpet, there were African masks, a carved Japanese screen, a batik from China that looked antique, a low chaise upholstered in a Marimekko print from Finland, and several dozen pieces on the walls, including a series of nude Barbie dolls mounted on a canvas and painted in various colors with headings scribbled around them in differing alphabets.

"Maybe the Barbies could stay," I said. "They look American."

Blass laughed loudly. "That's the only piece that's mine. Can you believe it took first prize at the Western States Biennale? The judges said it captured America's commercialization of the female form and how we export our twisted view of women to other cultures. Quite a load of bullshit, wouldn't you say? But one collector actually offered me ten thousand for it. Life is good when you're an artist. But poor old Arthur here is a writer and can't get a word published, can you Horace?"

Horace looked at me with his turmeric eyes. "It's true. My work is crap like Freddie's. The difference is no one wants to buy it."

Blass had a triangular face with a sharp nose above the thin moustache. His high forehead was topped with prematurely gray hair combed casually back without a part. He had intelligent eyes, a great voice and very good posture. His outfit was more costume than clothes, but he actually looked good in it.

He offered to get me a second glass of champagne and Horace Arthur a single malt scotch if he would leave me alone. Horace agreed and he and Blass went to the bar. Freddie returned with my champagne, and I noticed it was in a freshly chilled flute. He flung his arm around my shoulder and said, "Let me show you around."

He did, and I was happy to confirm that Gerstner was not among the guests. Neither was Stella, but all the other beautiful people were, most of them dressed with élan if not flamboyance. Still, I could not bring myself to put the ascot back on.

The Frederick Blass Collection was not confined to his expansive living area. The bedrooms were packed with paintings, sculptures, photographs and collectibles ranging from antique dueling pistols to a working renaissance clavichord. Even the bathrooms had paintings. One had what appeared to be a genuine Degas—a nude in a bath, appropriately enough.

After the tour, Freddie guided me to Susannah.

"I think you know this stunning beauty," he said and excused himself to see to his other guests.

Susannah usually looks like the girl next door with her brown hair in a ponytail and dressed in her waitress' uniform of black slacks, a man's shirt and sensible shoes. For Blass' party, she wore a swishy emerald-green dress with spaghetti straps and her hair up to reveal shoulders that deserved the description of stunning.

"Well, Hubie, what do you think?"

"I think he's right. You look fantastic."

"Thanks, but what I meant is what do you think of Blass?"

"I like him. He's affable, bright and a great host."

"Yeah, he's quite a charmer."

I pulled her aside. "Listen, Suze, it's time for me to take that little stroll we talked about."

33

Susannah retrieved her cell phone from her purse and called a number she had called shortly before we arrived. She listened to ten rings then hung up.

I slipped out to the hall and then in to the stairwell. I didn't want to risk meeting anyone in the elevator. I climbed one flight and was happy to find the clay plug still in the bolt hole. Happy but not surprised. After all, the doors opened from the floors as they always had, and no one was likely to discover that they now also opened from the stairwell side because the residents who used the stairs wouldn't try to open a door back onto a floor other than the ground floor or the basement.

I eased the door open and saw no one in the hall. I walked directly to Gerstner's door and loided his lock.

I closed the door behind me and stood listening for any human sound. I heard none. I walked through the apartment and verified it was empty. Of course that had also been true the first time I was there, and the fear of having someone walk in on me again propelled me into action. But before I did what I came to do, I opened the door on the hutch and discovered the pot I had seen was gone.

Dang.

I removed my blazer and hung it over the arm of the couch. I pressed down on the Parsons table behind the couch firmly with both hands. It seemed sturdy enough for my one hundred and forty pounds, so I climbed onto it. I reached up and pushed a ceiling tile up out of its tracks. The Parsons table was the height of the couch back—perhaps three feet—and when added to my five feet and six inches, it put my eyes an inch above the suspended ceiling. I rose up on tippy toes and shone a small flashlight around the area above the tiles. I had decided after the first visit to the apartment that the only place the rest of the missing pots could be was above the suspended ceiling.

And what did I see when I looked up there? Wires, ducts, pipes and cobwebs. No pots.

I had left the pot in the hutch the first time because I had been interrupted. I'm not sure I would have taken it at any rate. I didn't want anyone to know I had been there. I wanted all the pots, not just one of them.

Resting on the ceiling tile next to me was a canister for a recessed light. I could see the edge of something behind it, so I reached around to see if I could tell what it was. Just as I touched it, a piercing boom assailed my ears, and I feared I had set off an explosion. Both my feet left the table but only one returned to it, and I crashed awkwardly to the floor.

A quick scan of the room from my position on the floor told me no one had walked in on me. I looked up at the ceiling and saw a sprinkler head next to the recessed light. That's what I had touched from the other side. It was not sprinkling, so I hadn't set it off.

I stood up warily and nothing gave way or hurt. Evidently, I hadn't broken anything, although I did have a scratch on my right arm under a tear in my shirt.

I climbed back onto the table. The tracks of the suspended ceiling hung from wire threaded through holes and cut with snips. My right arm had dragged across one as I fell.

I replaced the ceiling tile and dismounted somewhat less awkwardly than I had a minute earlier. I collected my coat and exited Gerstner's residence. I carried the coat because I didn't want to get blood on the inside of its sleeve.

When I arrived back at 1009, I tried the door and found it locked. Loiding it seemed like a bad idea since I knew not only that the owner was home, but also that he had several dozen guests. Anyway, Susannah and I had anticipated this possibility. I tapped on the door lightly and she let me in.

I was happy to see her. I was not happy to see Horace Arthur standing next to her.

"Where did you go?" he asked.

I opened my mouth to tell him it was none of his business when it occurred to me that being defensive would call more attention to my little sojourn than I wanted it to have, so I said, "I stepped outside for a smoke."

"Disgusting habit."

"I agree. I'm trying to quit by smoking two fewer cigarettes each week."

"I don't smell any tobacco."

I gave him what I hoped was another disarming smile. "See. It must be working."

"What happened to your arm?"

"I think I brushed against a nail on my way back here."

"Where were you smoking?" The guy was totally devoid of social grace.

Susannah grabbed my hand. "Come on, Hubie, buy me a drink," and she led me towards the bar.

"Bring me a scotch," Horace said.

"What happened?" Susannah whispered to me as we approached the bar.

"I fell off a table."

"Did you land on a drum? That was a really loud boom."

"You heard it down here?"

"Yes. I have to say, though, you don't look bad for someone who took such a loud fall."

"That wasn't me falling—that was what made me fall. The sound startled me and I jumped."

"Off a table?"

"Not exactly. I jumped straight up, but only one foot landed on the table when I came down, so I fell."

"You didn't break anything?"

"I don't think so."

"What was that noise?"

"I don't know. It didn't come from Gerstner's apartment. I thought maybe it came from down here."

She said it didn't. She had been by the door with a good view of the entire place and saw nothing.

I ask her to order me another champagne. I went to Blass' bathroom, washed the blood off my arm and covered the scratch with a Band-Aid I found in his medicine cabinet. I put my blazer back on and examined myself in the mirror. Then I took the ascot out and tried it on again. I felt a little like David Niven playing a cat burglar. "What the hell," I said aloud and walked back into the party.

34

Susannah smiled when she saw the ascot. She handed me a fresh champagne which no one could deny I had earned. Then she went to deliver another scotch to Horace while I went to mingle.

I introduced myself to a man in a black silk jogging suit and metallic silver running shoes who was looking at an R. C. Gorman painting of an Indian woman on her haunches. He said his name was Jack W-i-e-z-g-a. That's how he said it.

"You're wearing the state flag around your neck. Is that a protest of sorts?"

"What would I be protesting?"

"The treatment of the prisoners at Cerrillos? The lack of affordable housing in Santa Fe? How the hell should I know? It's your protest." He laughed and slapped me on my back. He had huge hands. His thinning silver hair was tucked behind his ears and was just long enough to curl up slightly in the back.

"It's not a protest. It's just a piece of clothing," I said.

"Sometimes a pipe is just a pipe," he said knowingly.

"Hmm."

"You a collector or a producer?" he inquired.

"Both I guess."

"Well, you're lucky. Most artists can't afford to be collectors. Look at this Gorman. The man's a genius. He drew those simple stylized curves, put sketchy feet on them and they caught on like the flu. Man's a millionaire, but look at this piece. Dated. Completely passé. The trick is not to produce great art. The trick is to produce it at the right time. Timing is everything. If Andy Warhol had done the soup can ten years earlier or later, he wouldn't have enjoyed even his own fifteen minutes of fame."

"I see what you mean," I said, although I didn't.

"What's your medium?"

"Clay."

"Dated. Completely passé. I do colossal oils, also dated and completely passé. But what can you do? You have to follow your own artistic drive. You can't control timing. And you need good representation, but art dealers are all assholes."

"Hmm."

"Where do you display?"

"Uh, well I—"

"Nowhere. Just what I thought. Nobody shows clay these days. Dated. Completely—"

Passé, I said under my breath as he said it out loud.

"Maybe you could show here," I ventured.

"With Freddie? You must be joking."

"You have to admit the place looks better than most galleries."

"Sure it does. He charges a fortune."

"I don't get it."

"You think all this stuff is his? It's on consignment. Not the Gormans, O'Keeffes and all that middle-class pabulum, but all the works by people you've never heard of, poor slobs hoping to become the Next Big Thing."

"You mean this really is a gallery?"

"More of a fencing operation with the cut he takes. Why do you think he invites the rich and famous to the parties? He hopes to sell them something, that's why."

"But some of this work looks quite good."

"Like what?" he challenged.

"I understand the Barbie doll thing won a prize."

"The Western States Biennale? What a farce. I think Blass started it along with a few other wheeler-dealers hoping to play off the real Biennale. If he won a prize, it's probably because he was the judge."

"Why do you come to his parties?"

"Good-looking women and free booze."

"Ah."

Susannah rescued me from Wiezga, and we said goodnight to Blass and headed to the door which was being guarded again by Bertha Zell. "Call me and we'll have lunch," she said to me, and then she formed a phone by sticking out her thumb and pinkie and curling up her other three fingers. She waggled the hand by her ear and broke into giggles.

"I'll come along, too," volunteered Arthur.

I was telling Susannah in the elevator that despite the weird guests and falling off a table, I enjoyed the party.

"You should get out more often."

She was right. I usually decline invitations because I think I won't enjoy the people I'll have to mingle with. But when I do go out, I usually end up enjoying it. Even being around Arthur wasn't all that bad, something to laugh about later.

Then the elevator stopped on the fourth floor, and guess who got in?

To paraphrase Bogart, "Of all the elevators in all the buildings, she had to walk in to mine." But it wasn't as big a coincidence as meeting an old girlfriend in Casablanca, was it? After all, she lived in the building. And on that floor.

"Hubert!" said Stella. Then she looked at Susannah. "And who are you?"

"I'm Susannah," she said and extended her hand.

"And I'll bet you came from Alabama with a banjo on your knee. I'm Stella, but of course you already know that."

Susannah's big eyes were suddenly smaller, and as she opened her mouth to say something, I had the sinking feeling an ugly scene was about to ensue, but Stella continued talking.

"That's a lovely gown, Susannah."

"Thank you."

"You're not the wife, are you?"

"The wife?"

"I guess not," said Stella, "you're too young."

The elevator door opened on the first floor. "This is where we get off," I said and pushed Susannah towards the lobby.

"I'm going to the basement to get my car. I have to go to work." As the door closed, she smiled and said, "Call me, Hubert."

35

"What was that wife crack about, Hubert?"

"She thinks I'm married."

"Why would she think that?"

"Because I told her I was."

"Why did you do that? Because if it was to keep her from coming on to you, it didn't work."

"Geez, Suze, are you angry about something?"

She let out a long breath and stared out the window of the Bronco. "Sorry. I don't like her and I was taking it out on you."

"That's okay. I felt the same way when I first met her. Come to think of it, it was in that same elevator. She was asking me a bunch of impertinent questions about my wrinkled clothes and unshaven face, and I thought 'what a pushy broad'. I know you're not supposed to say 'broad', but that's the phrase that came to mind, and I—"

"Well, she is a pushy broad. And why the hell does she think everyone knows her? And where does she work that she goes in at three in the afternoon one day and eleven o'clock at night the next?"

"Maybe she's a famous surgeon on her way to the hospital."

She looked at me like I was an idiot. "Just because she's good at anatomy doesn't mean she learned it in med school. And surgeons don't wear those clothes and that makeup."

"Oh."

"Well, forget about her. Tell me what happened upstairs."

I did and she asked me where I thought the pot had gone.

"I assume it's now with the others. Maybe he's been selling them off one at a time and that was the last one."

"In one of the Mrs. Pollifax mysteries, a burglar arrives just as another one is leaving. Maybe that's what happened. Maybe another burglar got there before you. Was anything else missing other than the pot?"

"Who is Mrs. Pollifax?"

"She's a grandmother in New Jersey who works part time for the CIA."

"Well, that's certainly plausible."

"There's no need to be sarcastic. It could happen. The CIA does some weird things."

"You've got a point. But I don't think two burglars hitting the same apartment in a high security building on the same night is very likely. On the other hand, given the rogue's gallery at the party, maybe someone else seized the opportunity to pop upstairs and take the pot. Did anyone else leave and come back?"

"I don't think so. I was by the door the whole time and . . . oh, you're joking, right?"

"Right. Anyway, it doesn't matter. The pot is just as gone whether Gerstner or someone else took it." I pulled up in front of her apartment. "It's so frustrating. I proved Masoir's suspicion was right by finding one of the Ma pots in Gerstner's apartment, but there's nothing I can do about it. I don't know which frustrates me most, the fact that he got away with it, or the fact that I lost the chance for a lot of money."

"You don't think you can find the pots somewhere else?"

"I don't know where to look."

"How about that cabin in the mountains that you don't know if Gerstner has?" she said and we both laughed.

Then I thought about it. "You might be on to something. Remember how I told you the apartment seemed like a temporary rental with so few things in it?"

She nodded.

"Well, maybe he's in the process of moving. Maybe he still has all the pots at his new location."

"How would you find out where that is?"

"Call information?"

36

But the next morning I slept late, and by the time I finally got up, it was too late to call information because I had to call my lawyer first.

I walked groggily into the shop in response to a banging on my door and saw one of Albuquerque's finest, Detective Whit Fletcher, waiting to be admitted. Well, maybe "finest" is stretching it a bit. I started to walk over to the door then remembered the whiz-bang lock Tristan had installed, so I picked up the remote and aimed it at the door.

But I didn't push the button immediately. I wished the remote could activate a sign telling him to go away. But of course you can't tell the police to go away, so I pushed the button, and a buzzing noise came from the door.

Whit just stood there. He did not look amused. I motioned him to come in, and he turned the knob and did so.

"You mistake me for a television, Hubert?"

"Huh?" Then I looked down at the remote in my hand. "Oh. That's how I open the door now."

"Ain't technology great? I'm surprised to find you here."

"I live here, Whit. Where else would I be?"

"Making a getaway. But maybe you didn't realize we already placed you at the murder scene."

My pulse sped up. "What murder scene?"

"That fancy building downtown with the doormen in those uniforms, they look like South American generals. You were there, weren't you?"

"Yes, I was, but I didn't murder anyone."

"What was you doin' there?"

"I was at a party."

"What hours were you at this party?"

"I don't know exactly. I'd say from a little after seven until around eleven."

"Anyone see you there?"

"Yes, dozens of people," I answered in a tone of satisfaction.

"Is that so? I'd guess they'd be the same ones saw you slip out of the party and come back fifteen minutes later."

Oops. Now I felt a little perspiration to go with the elevated heart rate. "Well, I certainly didn't go out to murder anybody."

"What did you go out to do?"

"I went out for a cigarette."

"That's odd, ain't it? Me knowin' you all these years and never knowin' you smoked."

"Well, it's not the sort of thing you advertise. I'm not very proud of it, but sometimes I get an urge I can't resist."

"And you didn't want to smoke in your guest's apartment, so you went somewhere else."

"That's right."

"Where?"

"Where?"

"That's right, where?"

I didn't want to say out in the hall because for all I knew other guests or other residents on the tenth floor had been coming and going while I was upstairs and they might tell the police I wasn't in the hall. I wasn't worried about a murder charge, but I was worried about a breaking and entering charge. See, I had the idea that you should be more concerned about a crime you actually committed than about one you didn't. Naïve of me, wasn't it?

"I was in the stairwell."

Fletcher brushed his hair away from his eyes with a meaty hand. "Did you know the police have the authority to enforce the fire code? Most people don't know that. They think only the fire department can do that."

"Hmm."

"And did you know the fire code requires doors to a stairwell in a residential building to operate only from the side where the residences are?"

"No, I didn't know that." I was developing a queasy stomach to go with my other symptoms.

"Yep, it's true. And I'd say that building is in violation of the code, because we know you came back to the party, and I don't know how you coulda done that if the doors wouldn't open from the stairwell where you was having a smoke."

164

"Oh, that's easy to explain. I held the door slightly ajar so I could get back in."

I felt good I had enough wits about me to handle that question. I wish I'd had enough to remember something else about the stairwell.

"I guess that would work, holdin' the door, but you didn't need to. You coulda let go and still got back in because the lock was jammed up with a piece of clay."

He took it out of his pocket and placed it on my counter. I stared at it and thought of Stella. Then I quickly got my mind back on the matter at hand and wondered if unfired clay would take a fingerprint.

"You ever see anything like that before?"

"You know I make pots. I've seen all sorts of clay in all sorts of shapes."

"Would this particular piece of clay be yours?"

"I don't know. Clay is clay," I said and thought to myself that sometimes a pipe is just a pipe, whatever the hell that means. I thought it had to do with either Magritte or Freud.

Focus, I told myself. It didn't matter that they found the clay. They couldn't place me at the scene of a murder, so I was safe so long as they didn't bring up the breaking and entering thing. Then it hit me—that was the noise. It was a gunshot. Someone had been murdered while I was in Gerstner's apartment. Oh great, I thought, my alibi for not being at the murder site was that I was somewhere else committing a felony.

But you already know my thinking was wrong, don't you? Rational all right, but wrong. You've figured out what came next, right? Sure you have. If Fletcher had accepted my explanation, I wouldn't be relating the rest of this conversation, would I?

"I think you knew a fella name of Gerstner, didn't you, Hubert? Seems to me he was the one kicked you out of the University. I guess some people might call that motive."

"Gerstner was murdered?"

He looked inside a little notebook. "That's what it says here. Gerstner. Ognan Gerstner. What the hell kinda name is Ognan?"

"It's Slavic."

I had looked it up after Susannah asked about it. I already knew it was Slavic, but I wondered if it meant anything. Just the sort of thing Susannah would say illustrates my desire to accumulate useless knowledge. So I looked up Ognan and found out it means 'fire'.

"Well, I don't know where Gerstner was murdered, but I can prove I wasn't there."

He brushed his hair back again and stared at me. "If you don't know where it was, how can you prove you weren't there?"

"Tell me this. Was he shot?"

"In the head at close range."

"I thought so. I can prove I wasn't there because I heard the shot. I didn't know it was a shot at the time, but it must have been. And when I heard the shot, I was not with Gerstner."

"Who was you with?"

"No one."

"It'll be kinda hard to prove you was someplace if you was there alone."

"I know, but I think I might be able to do it." I was thinking I might have to admit to the breaking and entering in order to escape a murder charge. I hadn't stolen anything, and I have no criminal record, so maybe I could get off with no jail time. Hey, I was breaking in for a good cause. I wanted to return the pots to the Ma. My lawyer could play up that angle. I might even come out of it looking good, and who knows what it could do for sales. I was beginning to think I was home free.

"Okay, Hubert, Gerstner was murdered in his apartment. Now where is this other place you claim to have been?"

That's when I asked if I could call my lawyer.

"Might be a good idea. You can call him from downtown."

37

I refused to be questioned until my lawyer arrived, so I spent the time thinking about my plight.

I kept telling myself I had nothing to worry about. I hadn't killed Gerstner. If he had been killed in his apartment I'd been in, it must have been after I left. In that case, the noise I heard wasn't a gunshot after all. He had come home after I left, and someone else had come to his apartment and killed him. After they got the time sequence all straightened out, the police would realize I hadn't done it, and that would be the end of the matter.

If he had a second apartment, that would account for why 1101 seemed so empty. And it would mean that when Fletcher said Gerstner was killed in his apartment, he meant the other apartment. But Fletcher also said Rio Grande Lofts was the murder scene. Okay, no problem. Gerstner was moving to a different unit in the same building. All of a sudden I felt great. It was either a confusion about time or a confusion about place, and when the confusion was cleared up, the whole mess would be over.

Layton Kent, Esquire, finally showed up. When I complained about how long I'd been in custody, he said only an hour had passed since my call, and I couldn't dispute him since I wasn't wearing a watch.

Layton was. A massive gold one tucked in a watch pocket with a chain attached to a button of his vest.

"You must be the only man in Christendom who still wears a vest," I said.

"And you, my dear boy, are my only client who is frequently arrested for murder."

"I don't think I've been arrested. They didn't read me my rights."

"Do not attempt to practice law, Hubert. It makes you appear pompous."

"And you're not?"

"I'm an attorney. It's permitted."

"Can you get me out?"

"I already have. I swung by Judge Aragon's house to have him sign a little writ one of my paralegals drew up. We'll stop by your place for a coat and tie—you do own a coat and tie, do you not?— and then to the club for lunch."

"I don't want lunch. I want to go home."

"Nonsense. I need to ask a few questions in order to defend you properly should the gendarmes be so foolish as to pursue their interest in you as a suspect, and being away from my table at the lunch hour is inconsistent with my reputation."

I was getting a headache. I don't know why they call them 'splitting'. Mine felt like my head was being crushed together, not split apart. I followed Layton out to the curb where one of his paralegals waited with the Rolls Royce. The Rolls is one of his many ostentations, but I admit it felt good to slide onto the supple leather of the back seat and let the soft breeze from the air conditioner wisp away the police station smell.

Layton is probably right about reputation. He is widely considered to be the most influential man in Albuquerque. He knows everyone who is anyone, and quite a few people like me who are no one.

Mariella Kent is the Grande Dame of Albuquerque society. She sits on every board of any significance, and no fundraiser of any size is attempted without her appointment to the steering committee. She is reputed to be a descendant of the Duke who gave our fair city its unusual name. The Duke never set foot in the New World, but I suppose it is possible a member of his family may have done so.

Mariella's old money gave Layton's career a rocket boost when they married, but he has added to the pile considerably with his legal practice. He serves the legal needs of most wealthy Albuquerqueans, including many other prominent lawyers. He runs his practice with a bevy of paralegals and secretaries but no other attorneys.

In light of all this, you might wonder why Layton Kent would have me as a client. The answer is that the charming Mariella is a collector of Indian pottery, and I am her personal dealer. I don't know if Layton knows the background of some of the beautiful works in his sprawling *pueblo moderne*, but if he does, he has no doubt arranged for both himself and his wife to have what lawyers call plausible deniability.

Layton's table overlooks the 18th green at his club. He wouldn't know an eagle from a roadrunner, but he knows the players. As they finish their rounds, they come by his table to pay obeisance. He pointed me to my chair and took his own. A covey of staff appeared, picking up glasses and putting others down, placing napkins across our laps and uncorking Dom Perignon.

The waiter stood like a sentinel while Layton sipped the famous bubbly and signaled it fit to drink with a nod of his head. My glass was filled, and I took a sip. Dom Perignon is marginally better than New Mexico's own Gruet, but it costs ten times as much. On Layton's nickel, I was more than happy to sniff the yeasty nose and taste the dry effervescence of the most famous of all bubblies.

Layton was wearing a gray wool suit with an almost invisible nutmeg pinstripe. His shirt was zucchini green and he wore a knit tie the color of wet sand. There were stays in his collar and a diamond in his tie the size of a martini olive.

"We'll have the *truchas en terracotta*," he announced to the room at large. He took a small sip of champagne and leaned towards me. "Now tell me how you ended up in this enchilada."

I told him the whole story while he waved to golfers and diners. Several visited the table to squeeze his hand. No one kissed his ring.

Our fish arrived. The succulent trout was de-boned and placed on our plates. One bite of the perfectly cooked fish with its piñon pesto stuffing and for a brief moment I forgot about my legal troubles.

I feared Layton hadn't heard a word of my story, but he surprised me when it was over by summarizing the entire thing and asking a few pertinent questions. Then he dismissed me.

"Can someone give me a ride back to my place?"

"Dear boy, I run a law practice, not a taxi service." But when I walked outside, the Rolls was waiting.

38

I went straight to my hammock and fell asleep.

When I awoke, it wasn't yet five o'clock and I didn't feel like opening the shop, so I walked over to the church and sat on the *muro* like a zombie until I heard footsteps approach from behind.

"Wall, Youbird, you have come for confession?"

"Hello, Father. No, just to get some sun."

"Zo you did not kill Master Gerstner as it says on the radio?"

I shuddered at the fact my arrest had been broadcast. "I did not, so I have nothing to confess."

"Bot you know whot they say about confession."

"It's good for the soul?"

"Yas, and even batter for the priest. Iz our reality television."

When he stopped laughing, I asked him if he had known Gerstner.

The light went out of his eyes and he sat down next to me and

172

crossed himself. "Yas, I knew him. I had bad thoughts about him. May Got bless his soul."

"How did you know him, Father? Are you Czech?"

"No, Rusyn."

"I didn't know you were Russian."

"Not Russian, Youbird—Rusyn."

"Ah," I said, deciding to drop it. But it was too late.

"Mebbe you know us by a different name. We are also known as Rutherians."

"Rutherians," I repeated. "No, I've never heard that word."

"How about Ruthene?"

How about Rosicrucians I was tempted to say. "Sorry, no."

"Lemko?"

"I beg your pardon?"

"Have you heard of the Lemko? We are also called that."

I said no in what I hoped was an apologetic tone.

"Husal?"

How many names did these people have? I shook my head.

"Bojko?"

"No, I'm afraid I don't know that one either."

"Wahl," he said languidly, "it doss not matter. We are accustomed to this anonymity."

The good Father then launched into a dissertation on the sad history of a group of people who have many names and are unknown by all of them. During his recitative—Wagnerian in its length—I remained confident that if I continued to pay attention, the point of the narrative would eventually emerge.

I was mistaken.

The Rusyns consider themselves to be the indigenous inhabitants of Carpathia. Some of Carpathia is in Ukraine, which claims the Rusyns are Ukrainians and the Rusyn language is a backward dialect of Ukrainian. After the fall of the Iron Curtain, there was a movement among the Rusyns to have their own country but the split between the Czech Republic and Slovakia somehow undermined that pipe dream. I didn't see what that had to do with Ukraine, but at least the breakup of Czechoslovakia was something I had heard of, which is more than I can say for the rest of the story.

Evidently, the majority of the Rusyns have now turned their attention to achieving recognition and some degree of autonomy within Ukraine. To undermine that effort, the Ukrainian government has begun a "Rusyns are Ukrainians" propaganda campaign. This plays into the hands of a hard-line splinter group who insist on a Rusyn state and are alleged to be willing to achieve their goal by any means necessary.

After he had told me all that—you should be grateful I condensed it—he said, "Zo, Youbird, to make a long story short—"

"Too late for that," I interjected.

But he pressed forward. "There are Rusyn cabals around the world seeking to support minority rights for my people. There iz a cell even here, and Gerstner joined our little group of peaceful dreamers."

I was a little shaky on my geography. "Do the Carpathians extend in to Czechoslovakia?"

"Thar iz no Czechoslovakia, Youbird."

"Oh, right. So Gerstner was an ally."

"So we thought. Bot actually he wass a gawfer."

A golfer? I tried to imagine Gerstner in knickers and a porkpie hat. "He played golf?"

"Mebbe I do not say it right. Gawfer—a small animal who digs the ground."

I pondered it for a minute. "I think you mean a mole."

"A mole iz a spy?"

"No, a mole is a harmless little fellow whose name has come to be used in that way because he lives underground."

"Ah, then he woss a mole. Our little circle came to believe he woss in league with the Ukrainians."

"Did he do anything that might have gotten him killed?"

"Youbird, we are a harmless group of dreamers, a few refugees from a country that never exist. We raise a few dollars for the victims of the 1998 floods. No one kills anybody over the Rusyn question."

He shook his head.

I remained on the *muro* after Father Groaz left. I puzzled over whether the pot smashing was related to Gerstner in any way. By five o'clock I had reached the conclusion I expected; namely, that I had no clue and wouldn't have known what to do with a clue if I did have one. So I turned to something I do know about—Dos Hermanas.

The Dom Perignon hadn't completely worn off despite the afternoon nap, so I was sipping my margarita slowly.

"I can't understand why the police think you murdered Gerstner," Susannah said.

"Well, I have a motive, I was in the building, I left the party for no good reason and the shot was heard while I was gone. Then I came back with blood on me. That's enough to make the suspect list."

"But you already explained how the murder had to be at a different time or place."

"I explained it to you, Suze, and to Layton. I didn't explain it to the police."

"Why not?"

"Because I was just digging myself into a hole, so I decided not to say anything else."

"Sounds like my father. He likes to say, 'When you find you're digging yourself into a hole, the first thing to do is stop digging'."

"Which is what I did. Let Layton worry about it."

"So now what?"

"I wait for a call from Layton telling me everything is okay."

She took a sip of her margarita and tilted her head back to catch the sun's rays. The air was cold but the sun was warm and we were back on the west veranda.

"What about the pots?" she asked the sky.

"Being arrested for murder doesn't lessen my need for money. I've still got mortgage payments and rental payments. I still have nothing to sell in one of the shops. Consuela may still need a kidney transplant. And now I've got a big legal fee to boot."

"It can't be that much, can it?"

"Oh, it can mount up pretty fast. Layton charges five hundred dollars an hour."

"Geez, that's a million a year."

"That's a pretty fast calculation for someone who claims she's not good in math. But he makes a lot more than that. You don't think he bills only two thousand hours a year, do you?"

39

On Friday morning I went to see a hatter named Vlade Glastoc.

I didn't know there were still hatters. I figured hats all came from factories these days, but we have a hatter in Albuquerque, and he has a shop on Silver a block west of the train station where he can make any sort of hat you want, and it fits you perfectly because he measures your head and tailors it right to your measurements. Or, maybe that should be 'hatters' it right to your measurements. And it is measurements—plural. Turns out a proper hat size is more than just the circumference of your noggin.

"Your head is perfectly sized for your height," he told me after he had measured mine the normal way as well as from ear to ear over the top and from my eyebrows to the base of the back of my skull.

"No one knows how to size a hat these days," Mr. Glastoc lamented. He centered a plaster of Paris head on the counter and lowered a metal loop onto its forehead. "You see how that rests perfectly on the head?"

"It certainly does," I said admiringly.

"It does not," he contradicted. "It *appears* to rest properly because it is at the wrong angle. Observe," he said like a magician, and tilted the hoop. "Now you see it is too small." Then he tilted the loop in the other direction. "Now behold—it is too large."

"Amazing."

He nodded appreciatively. He was a small man with small eyes. I don't know if he had the right sized head—it seemed a smidgen small to my untrained eye. He made up for his head size with a lot of hair, jet black and combed straight back without a part. He spoke faintly accented English and his word order was unidiomatic in a few cases, so I guessed he was foreign born. And it turned out I was correct.

Of course my getting it right may have been aided by his given name being Vlade, not a common naming choice for American parents. And I was also aided by the fact that Father Groaz had told me Glastoc was Rusyn.

I hadn't told Glastoc that. I wanted information from him, but I didn't want him to know what I wanted. I didn't know what side he was on. In fact, I didn't even know what sides there were.

"That's an attractive flag," I said to him.

He glanced at the flag on the headband catch of a natty hat I would have described as Tyrolean. I expected him to say something like, "Yes, that is the Rusyn flag," thus providing an entrée for a conversation on the topic. Instead, he grunted and asked me what style of hat I had in mind.

I told him the one with the interesting flag appealed to me.

"All wrong for you. A hat like that is worn by large men as a minor decoration. On you it would only make you look smaller."

"Oh. Well, how about a larger hat with the same headband. I really like that flag. What country did you say it's from?"

"I didn't say. Here, try this one." He handed me a Western straw hat without a band.

"I don't like straw. And I definitely want a headband."

He produced another one from under the counter. "Try this."

It was an updated version of the homburg. I hated it before even trying it on.

We went around like this for a while, me bringing up the headband and the flag and him bringing up more hats. Finally, he produced a soft felt number with a brim wide enough to give protection from the sun and a crown low enough to avoid making it seem like I was trying to look taller. It had an attractive band made of dark green ribbon, and it felt good in my hand and even better on my head.

"I'll take this one if you can put that headband on it," I said, pointing again to the Tyrolean model.

"I can't sell you this one. It doesn't fit you properly."

"But it feels perfect."

"The one I make will feel even better. Besides, the one you hold has been too long in the shop. You will like better the one I make just for you."

"Okay, but what about the headband?"

He shrugged. "If you like it, I can make one like it for this hat, but I don't think it is appropriate."

"Maybe you're right. I don't even recognize the flag. It could be some terrorist regime for all I know."

Whereupon his small eyes grew even smaller, and he told me about the flag.

40

The hat was ready on Monday and I wore it to Dos Hermanas.

"Wow! First an ascot and now a fedora. You're becoming sartorially splendid."

"You think it looks good?"

"It looks great."

I took it off and hung it on the back of an empty chair. "I feel sort of self-conscious wearing it. Men don't wear hats anymore."

"My father always wears a hat."

"He wears cowboy hats. That's not the same."

"So you can be different. Where in the world did you find it?"

"I got it from Vlade Glastoc."

"You went to Russia over the weekend?"

I gave her a blank look.

"Well? Isn't Vladivostok in Russia?"

"Not Vladivostok. Vlade Glastoc. It's a name."

"Of someone who sells hats?"

"He makes them."

"But he's not in Russia?"

"No, he's right here in Albuquerque."

"I didn't know we had a milliner in town."

"Actually, I think he's a hatter."

"Why? Is he mad?"

"I wouldn't go quite that far. A bit eccentric perhaps."

"Well, what would you expect with a name like Glady Vlasnost? What kind of name is that?"

"It's Vlade Glastoc. And it's Rusyn."

"So he could be from Vladivostok."

"He isn't Russian—he's Rusyn," I said, stressing the long 'u' in Rusyn.

"Oh, Rusyn. Why didn't you say so?"

"You've heard of them?"

"Sure. Andy Warhol was Rusyn. His name was really Andrin Vargola, but he anglicized it to Andy Warhol. I read that his family came from Carpathia. Where is that, Hubie?"

"I'm not certain. Some of it's in Ukraine."

"You mean 'The Ukraine'."

"I think they dropped the 'The'."

She seemed genuinely disappointed about that, so I ask her why it mattered.

"Which sounds better," she asked, "I went to Ukraine or I went to The Ukraine?"

"The latter, but that's just because we've always heard it that way."

"No, I think it's because 'Ukraine' starts with a vowel. Other countries all start with consonants, so they don't need a 'The'."

I puzzled over her bizarre theory for a few seconds then said, "Italy starts with a vowel, Argentina starts with a vowel, Uruguay—"

"Those don't count. Romance languages have vowels everywhere. But countries where they don't speak Spanish or Italian all start with consonants—Germany, Poland, Russia, Japan, Canada, Sweden, Norway, China . . . You want me to keep going?"

"How about the United States?" I said smugly. "It not only starts with a vowel, but it's the same one Ukraine starts with."

"Right, and the name of the country is The United States of America. See, Hubie, you have to have a 'The' before a country that starts with a vowel."

"Especially a 'u'," I said, relenting. "Why are we talking about this?"

"Because your hatter was from The Ukraine."

So I told her what Groaz had told me about the Rusyns, aka the Rutherians, the Lemko, the Husal and the Bojko, including the fact that Ognan Gerstner had joined their local group and was suspected of being a mole.

"So you think that may have something to do with Gerstner's death?"

"Father Groaz didn't think so, but ethnic conflicts in that part of the world have generated violence for centuries, so I wouldn't rule it out."

"So you wanted to find out what this Vlade Glasnost knew about Gerstner."

"Vlade Vlasnost . . . no, that's not right either. Never mind—let's just call him Vlad. And yes, I went to his shop to see what I could find out."

"So the hat was just a front."

"More of a top, actually. And I needed a hat anyway. Did you know skin cancer is a major problem for people who live here in Albuquerque?"

"Yeah, I knew that, Hubert. It kills way more people around here than drowning. Are you going to tell me what you found out or not?"

"I found out that the bottom of the Rusyn flag has five red mountain peaks, the top part is sky blue and in the middle is a yellow sun."

"That's all you got out of him?"

I shrugged. "That and the hat."

41

I removed the foil from a chilled bottle of Gruet and had the wire between finger and thumb. Six twists would loose the wire. Then two twists of the bottle—one always holds the cork steady while turning the bottle, not the other way round—would loose the cork, and my breakfast would be complete.

But the phone rang and it was Bertha Zell who said she was worried I might be down in the dumps after being arrested, so she wanted to cheer me up by inviting me to lunch at the Crystal Palate. Thinking lunch would involve wine or spirits, I returned the Gruet to the fridge and poured myself a glass of mango nectar instead. I ate breakfast with my back to the fridge to resist temptation.

The Crystal Palate is in an old storefront on Central just east of the University and seems to draw a good crowd from the faculty and those few students who don't think salt and grease are basic food groups. The windows look like they were painted by Peter Max, and crystals dangling from the ceiling cast rainbows around the room. Booths nest under hanging silk pyramidal tents. Bertha was sitting under one of them soaking up its energy.

"What do you think of the place?" she asked as I slid in across from her.

"It looks like it was decorated by Shirley MacLaine."

"You're not going to be stuffy are you?"

"Heavens no. I'm looking on this as an adventure. How's the food?"

"Healthy."

"That bad, huh?"

"You're not wearing your ascot."

"This seems more a bell-bottoms sort of place."

"You are going to be stuffy, aren't you," she laughed.

"I am not. And just to prove it to you, I'm prepared to buy you a glass of New Mexico's best champagne, Gruet *Blanc de Noir*."

She swept her hand up to her heart and said, "How gallant of you. Would you settle for a fruit smoothie?"

"I would not. I had mango nectar with breakfast, and I have a firm limit of one healthy drink per day."

Her hand slid down and her head slumped. "I would love some Gruet, Hubert, but they don't serve it here."

"All right, how about some genuine champagne from France?"

She shook her head.

"A crisp cava from Spain?"

She stared at me, forlorn.

"A prosecco from Italy?"

She hung her head.

I looked around the room at what the other diners were drinking and then back at her. "They don't serve alcohol, do they?"

She nodded. "It's an organic restaurant."

"Champagne is made from grapes. Aren't those organic?"

"They serve only health food."

"Even the Surgeon General now says drinking is good for you."

"In moderation," she pointed out.

"Well," I said truculently, "they could serve it in small glasses."

"Would you prefer to go somewhere else?"

"No," I said, pretending to be cheerful, "this will make the cocktail hour that much more enjoyable." I looked around for a waiter.

I didn't see one, but I did see Horace Arthur coming through the door. "On second thought," I said, "maybe we should go somewhere else."

But it was too late. He slid in beside Bertha and said, "This is the third place I've looked. I was beginning to think I wouldn't find you."

"Devoutly to be wished," I said under my breath.

"Have you decided what we're eating?" Arthur said.

"We?"

"I never order in restaurants. I'm no good at it."

"I haven't seen a waiter," I said.

"What?"

"I haven't seen a waiter," I repeated as if talking to a child.

Arthur threw up his hands. "Labyrinthitis," he offered by way of explanation.

"That probably explains why you couldn't find us."

Bertha laughed and Arthur said, "What?"

I shrugged and Arthur got up and signaled Bertha to do the same. When she did, he slid back in and signaled her to sit back down.

"The doctor says the worst is over. The dizziness and nausea have gone away, and the hearing loss is temporary." He looked at

Bertha and said, "It's not as severe in my left ear. That's why we switched."

"Drat. And here I thought it was because you wanted on the inside where you could cop a quick feel without being spotted."

He stared at her without comment.

"Arthur," I said, "why do you wear those horrible turquoise glasses?"

"They were on sale."

"And why does everyone call you by your last name?"

"Because it's also a first name, I suppose."

"Great," said Bertha. "Now that we've cleared up those matters, maybe we can order."

"I still don't see a waiter."

"They don't have them here. And if they did, they would be called waitpersons. We select from the menu board and then order at the counter."

The menu was written in pastel chalk and was difficult to read because of the glare off the white marker board and the crisscrossing lights from the crystals. The first menu item seemed to be either tofu scallops or tofu scallions, and I twisted my head several ways trying to make it out until I realized it didn't matter. I wasn't going to order anything made from tofu.

That eliminated half the menu. I was debating the vegetarian chili when a shadow darkened the menu board. I looked up to see yards of black cloth and the bottom of a scruffy beard. I couldn't see the head because of the tent, but I knew who it was.

"Hello, Father Groaz."

"Hallow, Youbird. And Hallow, Bertha."

"Hallow be thy name, Father," said Bertha. "Will you join us for lunch?"

187

"Thot's very kind," he said and squeezed in next to me, knocking the tent with his head and setting it swinging on its chain.

Bertha introduced Arthur who responded, incredulously, "Father Gonads?"

At first I thought he was making a crude reference to the recent scandals of the Church, but then Bertha leaned in to his left ear and shouted, "Groaz, Groaz!" Then she turned to the priest and said, "He has temporary hearing loss from labyrinthitis."

"He woss lost in a maze?"

A skinny girl in the next booth with a long horsey face, big eyes and a yard of midriff showing turned to us and said, "Sorry to interrupt, but a labyrinth is not a maze."

"What's the difference?" asked Bertha.

"What?" said Arthur.

The girl swung around to the end of our booth, placed her elbows on the table and fixed her gaze on Father Groaz. "You should know. You're a holy man."

"Waahl—" he started slowly, sounding uncertain.

"A maze is a problem," she said, "something to be solved. You have to avoid blind alleys and work your way out. But a labyrinth is unicursal. The way in is the way out. Its path leads you around and around and then out again. It is not a problem to be solved. It's a journey to be enjoyed. You see," and here she paused and looked at each of us in turn with big watery eyes, "the labyrinth is a metaphor for life's journey."

"Oh, brother," I muttered under my breath.

"Could we order now?" asked Arthur, and for once I felt in league with him.

"I have some literature if you would like to have it," said the girl.

"Why thank you," said Bertha, "I'd love to see it."

While the Priestess of the High Church of the Labyrinth dug in to her backpack for pamphlets, I tried again to read the menu board, a task made even more difficult after Father Groaz wedged me in the corner of the booth causing my sightline to pass through the frayed end of his beard. The white silk of the swinging tent above my head was creating a strobe effect and giving me motion sickness. I had to get something in my stomach. "I'm going to order," I said, and I pushed Groaz until he let me out.

I selected a poblano pepper stuffed with brown rice, raisins, and sautéed pumpkin for myself and a plate of hummus with pita chips and steamed broccoli for Arthur since he had announced he never knew what to order.

Evidently, everything was already cooked. After all, the object was health, not taste. I carried the food back to discover that Ms. Labyrinth had joined our table and she, Bertha and Groaz were discussing metaphysics.

Arthur had moved to the girl's table, and I joined him and gave him his food. He ate it with gusto, including even the steamed broccoli.

My dish was less successful. What I'd taken to be a poblano turned out to be a bell pepper, which would have been okay if it were crisp, but it had been steamed into mush. The brown rice tasted like alfalfa, and even the pumpkin was next to flavorless owing to the absence of salt. Of course salt is an inorganic chemical, so I guess they wouldn't use it. The paper plate and plastic fork further diminished my enthusiasm.

"Why did you want to have lunch with us?" Horace asked.

"Bertha invited me, remember?"

"Okay, then why did you come?"

I pushed the stuffed pepper aside and took a sip of my lavender and linden tea. "I'm not sure. I guess I could ask her about Frederick Blass."

"You want to know more about the man who stole your girlfriend?"

"She's not my girlfriend."

"Not now at any rate."

"She never was. She's my best friend."

"And you want to know whether Freddie's intentions are honorable?"

"Arthur, I can't tell whether you're flippant or serious. Anyway, I don't know what honorable intentions would mean these days."

"I've never known him to treat a woman badly."

"Thank you."

He raised my cup to his nose and smelled the tea. "Smells like soap. This is the first time I've ever had lunch with a murderer. I wonder if I might get a short story out of the event."

"I assume you're being flippant."

"I admit you don't seem the violent type, but you did have blood on you when you returned to the party. I told the police that."

Oh, great. "It was my blood."

"I suppose you were bleeding from a burn inflicted by your cigarette?"

Why was I having this conversation?

I started to take another sip of tea, but Arthur's comment about soap spooked me.

"I found out something interesting when the police interviewed me," he said.

"Oh," I said, trying not to sound too interested.

"Actually, I didn't find it out. I inferred it. You see, they asked me if I knew Gerstner, and I told them I did. We were on a couple of faculty committees together. So when I told them I knew him, they asked me if the word 'hub' had any special significance for Gerstner."

He stopped talking and stared at me through those ridiculous glasses.

"And did it?" I asked.

"Not that I know of."

"So what is it you found out?"

"Not found out—inferred. I figure he must have had "hub" on or near him. Maybe he wrote it out in blood as he died to leave a clue for the police."

"He was shot in the head at close range. I don't think he did any writing after that."

"God, you're a brutal beast. A story about you could rank right up there with Truman Capote's *In Cold Blood*. Will you give me an exclusive interview? I'll share the royalties with you."

"I didn't kill him."

"But what about the word 'hub'?"

"What about it?"

"Well, those *are* the first three letters of your name."

42

I was happy to see Miss Gladys after I returned from the Crystal Palate. She evidently hadn't heard about my arrest or considered it an unfit topic for genteel conversation because she didn't mention it. Instead, she offered me something called seven-layer Mexican dip. I always thought of dips as creamy concoctions served in small bowls and scooped out with chips or crackers. But seven-layer is evidently an entrée.

Miss Gladys' food provokes in me an approach/avoidance conflict. On the one hand, I'm curious to know what's in it, partly because I like to know what I'm eating and partly because hearing her describe her concoctions is delightfully entertaining. On the other hand, her explanations of the ingredients often leave me longing for the blissful ignorance I enjoyed before asking.

I fancy myself something of an expert on Mexican food, a rich and varied cuisine that I'm certain contains no seven-layer dip. So I had to ask.

"Oh, this one's as easy as falling off a log. You just spread one can of refried beans on the bottom of a two-quart casserole dish. That's layer number one. Then you cover that with two cans of Fritos bean dip, two plastic packages of guacamole dip, one sixteen ounce tub of sour cream, a thin layer of mayonnaise and a package of taco seasoning. Cover that with shredded cheddar cheese then spread several cans of sliced black olives. It usually takes four of those little cans they come in. Then top it all off with chopped tomatoes and green onions."

"Miss Gladys, I believe your seven-layer dip has ten layers."

"Oh, pshaw! Did I mention that the mayo and the taco seasoning are combined together before you spread them?"

"No. So now you're down to nine layers."

"My goodness. Let me see. Oh, you must be counting the tomatoes and green onions as two layers, but it's really only one because they're chopped up together."

"That's eight."

She pinched her ear and looked to be in deep thought. Meanwhile, I had taken the liberty of spooning out a small portion since she was distracted from that duty she normally performs with gusto. As you know by now, Miss Gladys' units of kitchen measurements are not in teaspoons, cups or pinches, but in boxes, cans and bags. This dish at least had two fresh ingredients, and aside from the mayonnaise, the sour cream, and all the unknown additives in canned and processed food, it didn't seem unhealthy enough to warrant alerting the Surgeon General. Especially since I did not have a Miss Gladys-sized portion.

She perked up. "I've got it! You can count the refried beans and the bean dip as a single layer. Why, I suppose you could even stir them together before you started. What do you think? Would that improve the dish?"

I told her it was perfect as it was.

She departed with her dirty dishes after trying unsuccessfully to force a second helping on me. I headed over to Dos Hermanas.

Angie sashayed up to the table and placed fresh green margaritas in front of us.

Susannah must have seen me looking at Angie walking away, because she said, "She's attractive isn't she?"

"So are you."

"Yeah, I know—the girl next door, healthy looking. But when I see someone as lissome as Angie, I don't feel healthy, I feel clunky."

I recited a few lines of poetry:

I think it very nice
for ladies to be lissome
But not so much that you cut yourself
if you happen to embrace or kissome

"Ogden Nash?"

"Yeah, but I'm not sure I got it exactly right."

"Guess, what? The police were waiting for me after the lunch shift today, and they interviewed me about the party."

"Yeah, they also interviewed Horace Arthur."

"How do you know that?"

I took a sip of my margarita and told Susannah about lunch with Bertha Zell.

"And she invited Arthur?"

"No. He was going from restaurant to restaurant trying to find us."

"That sounds about right. Where did you eat?"

"The Crystal Palate. Father Groaz came in shortly after Arthur found us, and Bertha invited him to join us. Then there was a girl in the next booth who started talking to us about labyrinths, and Bertha invited her to the table as well."

"Should I ask about labyrinths?"

I shook my head.

"I didn't think so. I've eaten at Crystal Palate. The food's not as bad as you think it will be."

"Mine was. In fact, it was so bad that I was actually happy to see Miss Gladys when I got back."

"What was it this time?"

"Seven-layer Mexican dip."

"Ooh, I like that. My mother makes it all the time."

I felt as though there was an entire cuisine out there featuring things like seven-layer dip and King Ranch chicken, and I was the only person in America who didn't know about it.

"You may not like the food," she said, "but the name's catchy. It must be a pun on Crystal Palace."

"Yeah, but why? What connection is there between an exhibition hall in Victorian England and a health food place in Albuquerque?"

She stared at me blankly. "I meant the restaurant in California run by Buck Owens."

Now I stared at her blankly.

"Different generations," she said.

"So what did the police ask you?"

"Just what you'd expect—when did we arrive, when did we leave, why did you leave the party for a while, how were you acting after you came back, did I see blood on you, stuff like that."

"They probably drew up a list of questions to ask everyone. Arthur told them he saw blood on me."

"I told them that, too. I figured someone else would tell them, and if I said I didn't see it, they'd know I was lying, and that would make them even more suspicious of you."

"Good thinking."

"But I also told them I saw the cut on your arm, so the blood obviously was your own."

"What did they say to that?"

"Nothing. They just asked the questions and wrote down my answers."

"What did you say about why I left the party?"

She gave me a big smile. "I think I was pretty clever with that one. I remembered you told Arthur you'd gone out for a cigarette, so I told them what I heard you say to him. Then they asked me what you'd said to me about it, and I said you hadn't told me why you went out and I hadn't asked. So they asked me if I knew you smoked, and I said I'd never seen you smoke, but we spend most of our time in a restaurant where it's not allowed, so maybe you do have a cigarette now and again."

"Thanks, Suze. You done good."

"You haven't heard the best part. After they finished with their questions, they asked me if there was anything I remembered that might be helpful, so I told them that when you came back, you asked me what that loud noise was because you thought it must have come from Freddie's apartment."

"Excellent."

"Thanks. But they know we're friends, so I don't know if they believed me."

"Well, it's the truth. And the source of that noise may be the key to figuring out who killed Gerstner. It didn't come from 1101 and it didn't come from Freddie's, so my theory that Gerstner was changing apartments in the building must be right, and the shot came from his new apartment. Did they ask you if you knew Gerstner?"

She nodded. "I told him I'd heard of him but never met him."

"So they didn't ask anything else about him?"

"No, why?"

"Because Arthur did know him, and they asked him if the word 'hub' had any special significance to Gerstner."

Of course the mention of a possible clue plunged Susannah into her mystery mode. "Hmm. Doesn't sound like a word that would be very useful as a clue. Could be part of a wheel, could be any place with a lot of activity . . . Hey, some of the students at UNM call the cafeteria The Hub. You think that's it?"

"I have no idea, but I know what Arthur thought it was."

"What?"

"The first three letters of my name."

She stared at me for a few moments then said, "Like maybe Gerstner was trying to write his killer's name out in blood but died before he got to the fourth letter?"

"That's what Arthur surmised."

"Do you think the police will think Gerstner was trying to write your name?"

"Fletcher told me he was shot in the head at close range. That probably rules out writing anything afterwards. What's more likely is he had a piece of paper in his pocket or wallet with 'hub' written on it. And why would anyone think that's part of a name?"

"So you're not worried?"

"I'll be worried until they catch the murderer, but three random letters don't worry me."

I could sense she was disappointed. There's nothing she likes better than a mystery. She sat there brooding for a minute and then brightened and said, "Maybe 'hub' has something to do with the pots."

"Like what?"

"I don't know. You're the potter."

"I can't think of any connection between pots and hubs. I'll let the police figure out if 'hub' is a clue. I have my own agenda—finding any of those pots that haven't been sold."

"Because you'd like to see the originals returned to the Ma," she said with a sly smile.

"I would like that."

"And you're fascinated by old pots."

"Yes."

"And you'd like to take a stab at copying them."

"Absolutely."

"But mostly it's the money," she said.

We smiled at each other and clinked our glasses together.

"Another thing," I added, "is I won't have to worry about Gerstner walking in on me."

"That's cold, Hubie."

"Maybe, but you know what he is now?"

"What?"

Her humor had put me in a mischievous mood. "He's a cancelled Czech."

She groaned.

I shrugged. "I never did him any harm when he was alive, and I can't hurt him now. The fact is he kept those pots after saying he was going to return them. Now he's no longer around to hide them or claim them, so it really is finders keepers."

"What if he sold them?"

"Then it's too late, but I have to start with the hypothesis that he still had some of them. And there's another thing."

"Oh?"

"There was something strange about the design on the pot I saw in Gerstner's apartment. I don't know what it was, but something was different, out of place. It could be significant if I can figure it out."

"What's your first move?"

"I need to go back to Gerstner's apartment and search it more thoroughly."

"But you said you did a thorough search the first time."

"I did. But all I was doing then was searching places big enough to hold a pot. Now I want to search everywhere. And since there's very little chance of anyone coming in, I can take my time and do just that."

"What if the police come in?"

"I'm sure they've finished everything they need to do."

"But won't there be crime tape or whatever they call it?"

"Hmm. I hadn't thought of that."

"Maybe you should get Fletcher to go with you."

"Now I *really* hadn't thought of that. There may be money in it, so he might just do it."

43

As we headed for the entrance to Rio Grande Lofts, Fletcher asked me to keep our task as quick as possible since his visit was not official. Luckily, Rawlings was not on duty.

Fletcher showed his badge to the doorman and told him we were going up for some further forensic work in 1101.

"Will you need a key?"

"That won't be necessary," I said before Whit could answer.

After we were in the elevator, Fletcher asked me, "You got a key to the place, Hubert?"

"No."

"Neither do I. It's bad enough me coming down here with a suspect. And I sure as hell wasn't about to be seen goin' in to the property room to get our key, so how you figurin' to get in?"

"You told me you wanted this visit to be quick, so I guessed you didn't want to hang around in the lobby while the doorman searched for the spare key and then maybe had you sign it out or something."

"Yeah, I don't need to be signing anything. But we still got to get in."

"Trust me."

"Trusting you puts acid in my stomach. But it usually puts a few dollars in my pocket, so do what you gotta do."

He ran a pocketknife between the door and the jamb neatly slicing all the yellow tape. When he finished, I took out my piece of plastic and loided the door.

"Jesus, Hubert, you really are a burglar."

I had given him most of the background. When he found out what the pots were worth, he agreed to go along with me. He started searching the apartment and I sat down and went through all the papers in the drawer of the hutch. I found what I thought I needed, his checkbook and some other papers of interest. Fletcher didn't find anything of note.

"Where's the chalk outline of the body?"

"We don't do that no more, Hubert. We got these photographers that take a bunch of pictures. You didn't kill him, did you?" It wasn't a question.

I shook my head.

"Well then you wouldn't know where he was. We found him slumped over on that couch."

I walked over and looked around. "There's not much blood."

"Geez, I guess all the detectives and the lab techs must have missed that, but thanks for pointin' it out to me."

"I just thought there would be more blood."

"Well, you're right. It bothered us at first, too. But take a look at that stain on the back of the couch. You see how it's sort of swirly? We figure there was more blood but the murderer wiped most of it off."

"Why would he do that?"

"How the hell would I know? Maybe the killer was a professional upholsterer and hated to see the couch ruined. Criminals do strange things. They ain't normal like me and you. Well, me anyway."

I showed him what I found and what I thought it meant.

"Well, I hope you're right for both our sakes. And remember, Hubert, I was never here. I'm just glad I didn't have to identify myself to the doorman. The badge was all it took. But he might remember me if he ever had to, so don't mess up."

Whit put fresh crime scene tape around the door. Then we walked to the elevator. The door opened before we could push the button, and guess who stepped out?

"Hubie! I knew you lived on this floor. I remember riding up with you the day we first met. What a mess you were." Then she turned to Whit and said, well you know what she said.

"Of course he knows you, Stella," I replied before Whit could say anything. "Everyone knows you. Stella, this is Gus Inchaustigui."

"Pleased to meet you, Gus. Hubert, do you have a minute to talk?"

"Sure, why don't we all get on the elevator and you and I can get off at four and Joseph can ride on down to the lobby."

Slick how I avoided having the conversation on the eleventh floor, wasn't it? I guess I could have pretended 1101 was my apartment, but she probably would have noticed the crime scene tape, not to mention that loiding my own door to get inside might have set off a few alarm bells in her head.

44

"Hubert, i don't think you've been completely honest with me."

"Why do you say that, Stella?"

"Because I asked Rawlings which apartment Hubert lives in and he said he didn't know any resident named Hubert. He asked me your last name, and of course I couldn't tell him because you never gave me your last name."

"You never gave me your last name, either."

She laughed. She had a very good laugh. "That's because you already knew my last name, silly. And then I saw you with another woman, and I thought maybe you have a relationship with her, and that's why you were a little hesitant at first the other day when I showed you how to iron."

That wasn't the only thing you showed me, I thought to myself. "She's just a friend," I said.

"Is that why she was here the other night wearing an evening dress? And you were wearing an ascot, which, by the way, looked really sexy. So I figured the two of you had been to that big party upstairs and then back to your apartment for a nightcap and . . . and what else, Hubert?"

"Nothing else, Stella. You're right about the party. She was invited to the party by someone she met over the internet, and she asked me to go along because . . . well, internet dating, you know?"

"Tacky."

"That's what I thought. Anyway, I wish I hadn't gone because someone was murdered in the building during the party, and the police thought I did it. They even arrested me."

"Well, I obviously know all about that. And everyone in the building is talking about it. That Frederick Blass is not too popular among the residents, always having big loud parties. Some people were saying he invited a murderer to our building, but I told them you didn't do it."

"How do you know I didn't do it?"

"I have inside information, silly," she said as she slid over closer to me. "Tell me about Susannah, Hubert."

"Really, we're just friends."

"I'm happy to hear that, because I'll tell you what I was thinking. I was thinking maybe you left your wife because of Susannah. But it really is the other way around? She left you for a younger man?"

"She did." Well, what else could I say? This didn't seem the time or place to set the record straight.

She scooted even closer to me on her couch. She smelled faintly of some exotic fruit like persimmon or guava. Or maybe it was passion fruit—that would make sense.

"I'm glad we had this talk, because I'm very attracted to you, and I'd hate to think you were leading me along."

"Oh, I'm definitely not doing that," I said honestly. I mean, who was leading whom here?

"Everyone imagines I have a terrific love life. I know I'm attractive, intelligent and charming, and of course what I do is considered glamorous by most people, although I can tell you it's extremely demanding work."

"I know it is. And the hours are terrible."

"You do understand. I knew you would. And because of the glamour of it all, I get a lot of men coming on to me, but usually they're not my type. In fact, some of them are weirdoes. That's why I'd never meet men over the internet. I'm sorry to speak ill of your friend Susannah, but I think computer dating is really tacky."

I muttered something in agreement.

"So I feel lucky, Hubert." She inched even closer. "I didn't have to go online to meet you. All I had to do was get on the elevator. Isn't that lucky, Hubert?"

"It is."

"Do you feel lucky, too?"

"Sure. I mean—"

Then her hands were all over me and her mouth was all over me, and once again my mind was not up to the task of thinking up a reason to resist, so I didn't.

45

Susannah plopped her drink onto the table and let her hands drop to her side. "She still doesn't know your last name?"

"When she said I hadn't given her my last name, I replied that she hadn't given me hers either, and she thought that was funny because everyone knows who she is. And then she started talking about herself."

"Including that she's attractive, intelligent and charming."

"Right. And then she started talking about how much she was attracted to me and how lucky she was—"

"I know, I know, then you got lucky too. But didn't you talk afterwards?"

"Umm . . . well, I fell asleep."

Susannah laughed. "Well, I guess it's nice to know you're a typical male."

"When I woke up, she was gone. She left me a note saying she'd gone to work."

"Geez. What does that woman do?"

I waved to the dusky Angie and she acknowledged my refill request with a wide smile.

When she delivered it, I tasted it as usual to be sure it was as good as the last one. It was.

"Are you interested in what we found in Gerstner's apartment, Suze, or are your interests purely prurient?"

"I have no interest in that woman, prurient or otherwise. I just find it amazing that after you spend the night in a parking garage, a gorgeous woman happens to get on the elevator with you, you feed her a ridiculous line about your wife leaving you for a younger man, and the next thing you know she's giving you nude ironing lessons. Meanwhile, I'm reduced to using online services to meet a man."

"You did meet a man, and at least you know what sort of work he does."

"Yeah, that's true."

"So how's it progressing?"

"We have a date tonight. He's meeting me here."

I sensed a lack of enthusiasm. "You have some reservations about Freddie?"

"No. Well, maybe."

"He's handsome, witty and has a good position at the university. Throws a great party, too."

She nodded.

"So why the reservations?"

She pushed her glass around the tabletop in small circles. "Maybe he seems too good to be true. Is he suave or just slick? I don't know. He talks about art and fame and money . . . Maybe he went on line because he was treasure hunting."

"Then why select you? Did your message on the dating site say you were an heiress?"

"You know what it said. You thought it up."

Here came that queasy feeling again. "I'm not sure that using my crazy idea was—"

"Forget it. Tell me what you found in Gerstner's apartment."

I handed her one of the papers I'd taken from the apartment. She examined it and said, "It's a letter to Gerstner from a former student wanting a recommendation. Is this supposed to be a clue?"

"Look at the date on the postmark and the address on the letter."

"October 25. It's addressed to Gerstner at the University. So what?"

"He's got an office there, Suze. Maybe that's where the pots are."

"I don't know. Gerstner retired only four or five months ago. He probably still gets lots of mail there."

"Sure, but the address is Anthropology Hall, Room 204. Mail from people who didn't know he was retired would be addressed to the chairman's office on the first floor. I think they gave him an office to use after he retired. They do that sometimes if the retiree is still active in research."

"Yeah, they did that for Jack Wiezga. He has a studio in the fine arts building."

"Really? How's his work."

"Dated and passé."

"I thought that's what you would say."

"Really? Maybe I heard it somewhere."

"So why would they give him studio space?" I asked.

She shrugged.

Then another thought crossed my mind. "What do you know about Wiezga?"

"He paints big abstracts using house paint. My studio friends don't think much of his work, but they say he was good at teaching oil techniques."

"You know where he's from?"

"I think he got his degree somewhere in the Midwest. Illinois? Michigan?"

"No, I mean his ethnicity. What sort of name is Wiezga?"

"Somewhere in Eastern Europe. I remember it was a standing joke in the department that the only representational painting he ever did was of a flag after the fall of the Iron Curtain."

"Why was it a joke?"

"Because the painting is in the departmental gallery, so we had all seen it. It's called Red, Blue, and Yellow, and it looks nothing like a flag. I guess he'd been doing abstracts too long to make anything look like something."

"I think I need a map of Eastern Europe."

"Why this sudden interest in . . . oh, the Rusyns. You think Wiezga is involved?"

"I don't know what to think, but maybe there's a connection between Wiezga, Gerstner and Glastoc."

"So what's next?"

"Maybe I can learn something by snooping around in Anthropology Hall 204."

Susannah took a sip of her margarita and smiled at me. "You're going to burglarize the University again? You must still be trying to get even with them for kicking you out."

I smiled back at her. "I'm just trying to recover stolen property."

"When the police take back stolen property, that's called recovering it. When *you* take it back, that's called stealing."

"A technicality. If the pots are there, I intend to take them."

"Everyone in the building knows who you are. How will you get in?"

"Simple. I'll go when no one is there."

"When would . . . Oh, here's Frederick now."

He was standing by Angie, his chin up, his mane brushed casually back, a big smile showing perfect teeth. He wore pleated grey herringbone slacks and a dark blue cashmere sweater. And—can you believe it?—blue suede shoes to match the sweater. I would have looked and felt like a buffoon in that outfit, but on Freddie it actually looked quite natural. He strode over like a male model, gave me a manly handshake and locked his arm around Susannah.

We chatted for a few minutes—he told me he wanted to see my work, maybe show some of it in his loft—and then they left. The old Elvis disc, *Blue Suede Shoes*, started playing in my head. I let it spin because it was fun to hear it again.

46

The next morning around eleven, I drove up to the keypad at Rio Grande Lofts.

Except it wasn't there. The keypad, I mean. Rio Grande Lofts was right where it's always been. But where the keypad had been there was a slot for inserting a card. I sat there staring at it until a horn sounded behind me. Unfortunately, it was not friendly Wes, the retired cattle buyer. It was a no-nonsense guy in a Lexus who was unsympathetic when I told him I'd lost my card. He did allow me to back out. I drove to a parking space down the street and sat there thinking.

Then I drove to Duran Central Pharmacy and bought a hamburger with green chile. Yes, you can buy hamburgers with green chile in a pharmacy. Hey, it's Albuquerque.

I took the hamburger to Tristan's apartment. There was no yellow Post-It note on the door, so I let myself in and started making coffee and transferring the burger from the Styrofoam to a real plate.

I don't know whether the brewing coffee or the clinking dishes woke him. He stumbled in to the kitchen and I stuck a hot mug of coffee in his hand. He took a couple of sips then stepped over and lowered the blinds.

"God, it's bright in here," he said and then, "Thanks for the burger," when I placed it in front of him.

He took one bite and said, "Duran Central, right?" He knows food, takes after his uncle.

He demolished the burger, a quart of milk, and a pot of coffee.

"That was delicious, Uncle Hubert. What brings you by other than wanting to make sure I get fed?"

"I need to find out how exit gates in parking garages work."

He gave me a strange look. "Well, I'm not an expert, but I can give you a summary. There are different systems. You have a particular garage in mind?"

"I do."

"When you approach the exit gate, do you drive over a rubber hose or a metal plate?"

"No, only solid concrete."

"In that case, the gate is activated by the magnetic field of your car."

"So the reason it doesn't open when people approach it on foot is that people aren't made of metal."

"Exactly, although I suppose you could trigger it if you had enough metal on you. Or in you. Can you imagine it, having a metal hip or something and walking up to the gate and it swings open." He laughed at the prospect.

"Could a metal hip actually open it?"

"No, because they're made from titanium and it's non-ferrous. And even if the hip was made of iron, it's probably not big enough."

"So how much metal would it take?"

"Depends on the system. There are low field and high field detectors."

"I'm probably going to regret this, but can you explain the difference?"

"Without getting too technical, a high field detector works on the Hall effect, and it takes a pretty good chunk of metal to activate it. A normal car would activate it, no problem. But a bicycle wouldn't, and with all the molded plastic body parts in cars these days, some compacts might not trigger it. That's why a low field system is better. It works by sensing a disturbance in the earth's magnetic field. See, the earth's magnetic field is pretty weak, about half a gauss, so even a fairly small magnetic field like a bicycle can be detected."

"And how can you tell which system is present?"

"One glance at the circuitry would tell you. You want me to take a look at it?"

"Thanks, but I don't think that will be necessary."

I figured the idea I had would work on either system.

47

Susannah frequently has her book bag with her at Dos Hermanas because she leaves from there and goes directly to class. How she can learn art history after a few margaritas is an academic mystery.

That night she was putting the final touches on a paper. The image of the painting she had written about looked like an ancient icon you might find in an orthodox monastery adorned with an onion dome.

"You like your course in sacred art?" I asked as I settled in and waved for Angie.

"That was last semester. This semester I'm taking the seminar on the symbolist painters."

"As opposed to painters who don't use symbols?"

She cocked her head to one side. "I hadn't thought of that. I guess 'symbolist' wasn't a good word choice, but I can see how they chose it. They were artists who didn't like the realism of the nineteenth century and how it elevated the mundane and even the gritty. They thought painting should reflect only noble themes—spiritualism, principles, ideals, things like that."

Since I was planning larceny for the next morning, I felt unworthy to comment on principles and ideals. The image on her cover page looked to me like a traditional Russian painting of a saint, a girl or maybe a young boy with his head at an odd angle and surrounded by a gold halo, something that should probably be preserved for historical reasons but you wouldn't want hanging on your bedroom wall.

"So they went back to painting icons?" I asked.

"No. This one just happens to have that look because it's supposed to be Tzarevich Dmitry."

"Well, that certainly explains it."

She laughed and said, "He was the youngest son of Ivan the Terrible," and handed me the picture for a closer look.

He was a handsome young man, slightly effeminate with dark hair and long lashes. His right hand curled out from under a long white robe and gently touched his heart.

"He doesn't look like someone whose father's last name would be The Terrible."

She laughed again. "Don't you know the story? He was supposed to have been killed by Boris Godunov. Tchaikovsky wrote an opera about it."

"You know I don't like opera music." I looked at the typing under the painting. It read: Царевич Дмитри, 1899. "Was Uapebny whatever the name of the painter?"

"No, silly, that's the name of the painting—Tzarevich Dmitry. I typed it in the Russian alphabet because Casgrail is such a stickler. We have to put every title in its original language and God help you if you leave out the year."

"So I guess the artist's name is not pronounced Hectepob," I ventured. It was on the title page as Нестеров.

"It's Nesterov. You don't know Cyrillic, do you?"

"The only thing I know about the Russian alphabet is the 'P' makes an 'R' sound. And since Царевич is 'tsarevich', I assume the 'Ц' makes the 'Ts' sound in 'Tsar'."

"Or the 'Cz' sound in 'Czar'," she added.

Which gave me the opening to say, "Did you know the real cause of the Communist revolution was the peasants found out the Tsar and the Czar were the same person, and they thought no one should be allowed to hold that much power?"

She rolled her eyes and shook her head.

I glanced back down at the word Царевич and at the name of the painter—Nesterov in our alphabet, Нестеров in theirs.

48

I drove to the campus at ten o'clock on a Wednesday with classes in full swing. Students hustled between classes and of course no parking space was open. I pulled in to a loading zone in front of Anthropology Hall.

I visit the campus several times a month to use the library or attend lectures or recitals. I've even visited a few of my favorite professors in the business college. But as you might suspect, I hadn't been in Anthropology Hall since the day I was booted.

I remembered Susannah chastising me for walking to Rio Grande Lofts the first time I got in and asking me what I was planning to do with the pots if I'd found them. I was taking no chances this time. If any pots were in room 204, I was going to haul them away.

I was wearing a pair of torn and stained Levis I use in my workshop and a tan shirt I'd purchased for fifty cents at Goodwill especially for the occasion. It had a patch over the left pocket that said 'Pete'.

It felt a little odd walking in, but I didn't dwell on it and the feeling passed. I nodded at a student sitting at the reception desk. He returned my nod half-heartedly and returned to the book he was reading. I walked up the stairs, found 204 and loided the lock.

It was a typical faculty office, ten by twelve with a desk, desk chair, visitor chair, bookcases and file cabinet. I went through the desk and took a few papers that looked like they might be significant.

The bookshelves contained mostly outdated textbooks and back copies of journals. There were some reference works and a few trade books. I suppose a map to the hiding place of the pots might have been tucked between the pages of one of the books, but the odds were slim enough that I didn't bother looking.

The filing cabinet had the typical lock you see on filing cabinets, a keyhole in one of those oval steel buttons that locks all the drawers when pushed in, which it had been. I had no way of opening it given that my only lock trick is loiding, but I had prepared for this possibility.

I returned to the Bronco and got a hand truck. I drug it up the stairs to Gerstner's office where I strapped his file cabinet to it. Then I eased it down the stairs. The kid at the desk looked up and then went back to reading. I loaded the file cabinet in the back of the Bronco, thinking as I did that it was lucky Gerstner didn't have a big heavy safe. Then I drove home.

You might be thinking my actions were highly out of character, that I was taking quite a risk breaking in to Gerstner's office in broad daylight. You might also think that hauling his filing cabinet away was rather brazen, but I can tell you I was not the least bit nervous. Most universities are low security institutions. Anyone can walk on to a campus and more or less have the run of the place. Of course if someone saw you loiding a door, they might call security. They might even ask you what you were doing if they saw you loading a filing cabinet in to a beat up old Bronco, although I doubt it. But I wasn't concerned about any of that because other than the one student, I knew there was no one in the building. All classes in anthropology and archaeology had been cancelled for that morning, and all the faculty and staff who worked in that building were attending a memorial service across campus for Ognan Gerstner.

49

I drove home and hauled the filing cabinet to my patio.

The lock was sturdy but the cabinet was just a boxy tin can. I used a long-handle screwdriver to pry open the top drawer, then I reached inside and bent the vertical rod that allows the single lock to control all four drawers.

I spent a couple of hours going through the papers in the top three drawers. Most of them were of no value to anyone now that Gerstner was dead—old class lecture notes, correspondence with booksellers, programs from professional meetings and offprints of some of his articles. I put all of those in my kiva oven along with some piñon logs. It was cold in the shade of the patio.

There were some papers that might be useful back at the University, things like recent letters of recommendations that students might need and minutes of curriculum committee meetings. I stuffed those in to a couple of padded envelopes and addressed them to the Department of Anthropology and Archaeology at the University. I omitted the return address.

I kept a few more papers I thought might be helpful to me.

I put the blade of the screwdriver against the metal inventory tag on the filing cabinet and struck it with the heel of my hand. It flew off. The inventory tag, that is. My hand stayed on the end of my arm.

I picked the tag off the flagstone. It was light, some sort of aluminum alloy probably. I tossed it in the fire and watched it melt in to a little ball that shimmered and shimmied like mercury. Oddly, that helped me eventually figure out the whole Ma pot mystery.

Then I removed the tape, brown paper and bubble wrap from the three pots I'd found in the bottom drawer. I got almost the same feeling I get when I dig up old pots, a mixture of excitement and reverence. I held them in my hands and felt their heft and their curve. I wished I could have watched while the potter made them.

They were obviously part of a set—same size, shape and colors, but different designs. The pot I'd seen in Gerstner's hutch wasn't one of the three I found in the filing cabinet, but it belonged to the set. The varied designs had one thing in common, a stylized rendering of their pueblo with mountains in the background. The feeling I'd had when I saw the one in the hutch *déjà vued* me. You'd think after looking at thousands of pots over the course of twenty-five years, I'd be able to spot what was off kilter, but I couldn't.

I re-wrapped the pots and put them in a box in the Bronco. Then I drove to the post office where I mailed the two envelopes to the university and to the dump where I deposited the filing cabinet sans inventory tag.

My final stop was at my dentist's office. It was closed, but it didn't matter. I didn't need any dental work. I had called ahead and asked my dental hygienist to do me a favor, and she was waiting for me.

Sharice and I have more than a hygienist/patient relationship. We flirt with each other. Actually, she does most of the flirting. It's hard to reciprocate with her fingers in my mouth. I took her to lunch once and we had a good time, so I asked her out. But she said her boyfriend wouldn't approve, and then after my next appointment she said she didn't have that boyfriend anymore, but I was seeing someone else by that time, so we've never actually had a date. I don't know if she'd like me to ask her out again, or if she's content to leave it at the flirting stage. I don't know how I feel about it either. She's intelligent and attractive, but do I really want to date someone who scrapes my teeth?

We chatted amicably for a while after she did the favor for me. Then I stopped by the police station on the way home and asked Whit to give me a copy of the paper with the first three letters of my name on it, the one they'd found in Gerstner's wallet.

I took it outside and looked at it as I sat behind the wheel of my Bronco. Despite the cool air, the inside of the Bronco was toasty thanks to its expansive glass and the robust New Mexican sun. It felt a little strange being parked in front of the police station with three stolen pots in my vehicle, but the only people who knew they were stolen were the Ma, and I doubted they'd reported it to the Albuquerque Police Department.

The three letters on the paper the police found in Gerstner's wallet looked like this: нцв.

Definitely the first three letters of my name. They were typed, so I didn't think anyone was going to claim that Gerstner started to type my name but didn't have time to finish. Unless he was sitting at the typewriter when he was shot. Then I remembered people don't use typewriters anymore.

I noticed the little squiggle on the lower right of the 'n'. They call that a serif. I'd read a book that summer by Father Edward Catich called *The Origin of the Serif* in which he claims serifs originated in ancient Rome when they carved words in stone. The letter outlines were first brushed onto the stone to show the carvers where they went, and when the brush first hit the stone it would leave a narrow mark and then widen out as it was pressed down. The stone carvers were illiterate, so they blindly followed the brush marks and that's how we got serifs. I hadn't dared mention the book to Susannah for fear of the scolding I knew she'd give me.

50

I put the ma pot on the shelf, the wheel on slow and my hands in the clay. The pot conquered my potter's block. The clay rose under my gentle urging to the exact shape of its inspiration on the shelf.

I spent all afternoon experimenting with different slip mixes and couldn't find one I thought was right, so I limited myself to one margarita with Susannah and then drove west that night to the Rio Puerco and dug up some clay. Digging clay is not illegal, and it's ridiculous that I have to do it under cover of night, but if I'm caught digging anywhere, you know what the authorities will think.

I spent the next three days on the project and never opened the shop. When the copy was finished, I lined a box with bubble wrap and hauled the thing to Dos Hermanas. On the way, I happened to spot one of those pseudo-trolleys at the Old Town stop, and I saw the gorgeous Stella on it. I stood there gawking. I started laughing. Then I started looking forward to telling Susannah.

But when she saw me with the box, Susannah wanted to know

what was in it, so I showed her the Ma copy. She said it was beautiful. I agreed, but it wasn't conceit. The design was someone else's. All I did was copy it.

"I did pretty well with my project, too," she said and handed me the paper on Tsarevich Dmitri. Or Czarevich Dmitri. The professor had scrawled some nice comments and a big red A on the cover page right above the title.

I played with some of the Cyrillic letters in my head for a minute and it came to me, but I decided I had to find out what it meant before saying anything about it to Susannah.

"Now what?" she asked.

"Now I take the real pots to Martin's uncle to see what he can tell me about them."

I took a sip of my margarita. It was delicious. Being abstemious for a few days had whetted my thirst. Then I told Susannah I knew what sort of work the gorgeous Stella did, but I didn't say what it was. I took another sip of my drink.

"Well, are you going to tell me?"

"Ask me how I found out."

"Oh, brother. Okay, how did you find out?"

"I saw her on a trolley."

"She drives a trolley?"

I started laughing and couldn't stop.

"It's not that funny, Hubert."

"It is funny. The image of Stella wrestling the wheel of a fake trolley is hilarious. But no, she doesn't drive a trolley."

"She goes to work by trolley? That's not much of a clue. Anyone can ride to work in that thing, even a surgeon."

"She wasn't in the thing. She was on it."

"I don't get it. What's the difference?"

"When you're *in* the trolley, you're inside in a seat or hanging on to a strap. When you're *on* the trolley, you're outside. Well, *you* aren't outside, but your picture is. A real big picture right there on the side of the trolley."

"Oh, my God, she's Stella Ramsey, Channel 17's Roving Reporter?"

"One and the same."

"Unbelievable! You know what, she's right. Everyone does know who she is."

"Except us."

"Well you don't own a TV, so that's no surprise, and I'm in class most nights or in the library, but at least I know the name. Hubie! Every man in Albuquerque sees her on TV and wishes . . . well, you know, and here you've been rolling in the hay with her. That's fantastic."

"Maybe. But I don't think I can keep pretending I live in Rio Grande Lofts and have a wife that ran off with a younger man."

"You'll have to level with her. Tell her—"

But I didn't get to hear how I should do the leveling because Freddie arrived and Susannah left. I stayed and had another margarita.

When I got home, I called Tristan and asked him to make a videotape of Stella doing her reporting.

51

Jack Wiezga's studio in the Fine Arts Building was fifteen feet square with shelves on one wall and canvases leaning against the other three. The shelves were full of paint cans and brushes, and the floor was layered with paint splatters. It looked like one of his canvases except the composition was better.

"I see you're still using your clothes as a protest," he said by way of greeting.

I felt my neck to see if I had inadvertently worn my ascot, but of course it wasn't there. I gave him a blank look.

"The Rusyn flag," he said.

I removed my hat and eyed the headband. "So that's what that is."

"Playing dumb? Or is a flag sometimes just a flag?"

"Huh?"

"Glastoc called me after you left his store."

"Oh? What did he say?"

"He said that crazy pottery thief came by and tried to get information about the Rusyns, but all he would tell you about was the flag."

I decided to ignore the thief business. "How did he know me?"

"Your fifteen minutes of fame, Schuze. You were in the news in connection with Ognan Gerstner's death."

"I didn't kill him."

He shrugged. "Thank God someone did."

"Well, I'm not that someone. But I'm still a suspect, so I'm trying to find out who did."

"And you think a Rusyn might have done it?"

"You didn't think too highly of him."

His sloping brow slid down as his eyes narrowed. He tossed his brush in a can of turpentine and wiped his hands on his coveralls. Then he dug a pipe out of his pocket, filled it with tobacco and lit it. The smoke smelled like burning tires.

"Balkan Sobranie," I guessed.

"You know tobacco?"

"Not really. I had a roommate who smoked that my freshman year. No girl would go anywhere near the room."

He laughed. "Balkan Sobranie was a well-known female repellent. They don't make it anymore, but not for that reason." He held up the pipe and looked at it fondly. "This is straight latakia. It comes from Ukraine."

"Grown by Rusyns?"

"Rusyns live in the mountains to the north. The tobacco is grown in the lowlands of the south."

"You ever been there?"

"I was born in Michigan. Went to school there. Came here to teach. I don't even have a passport."

I took a piece of paper out of my pocket and handed it to him. On it were written three Cyrillic letters—НЦВ.

"Recognize this?"

He stared down at it for a long time. I didn't think he was studying it. He was trying to figure out how to respond.

When he finally looked up, his eyes were still narrow and his prominent jaw set. "Looks like the first three letters of your name."

"Is that the party line?"

He just stared at me, so I said, "The letters are Cyrillic."

"I don't know Cyrillic. Like I said, I don't even have a passport. Just a typical American."

"Have any theory about who killed Gerstner?"

"Maybe it was you after all."

52

I placed the pots on Martin's kitchen table, and his uncle's normally stoic countenance melted to reverence as he stared at them.

I lifted one of the pots, turning it to the part I wanted Martin to see.

"I knew there was something strange about these pots when I saw the first one, but it took me a long time to figure out what it is. This line represents the river. Behind that you see the stylized rectangles of a pueblo, and behind that the twin peaks."

I stopped talking while he took in what I'd said. After twenty seconds, he said, "So?"

"Look where the peaks are in relation to the pueblo."

"To the left. Is that supposed to mean something?"

"I once sold a pot your uncle made that differed from this one in only three ways. First, it was better crafted, but that's just a matter of technology. This pot is older and wasn't made on a modern wheel. Second, your uncle's pot didn't have this thick base. But the difference I think is significant is the location of the peaks. Your uncle put them to the right."

Martin took the pot from me and rotated it gently in his hand. Then he set it in front of his uncle and began to speak in their language. There was a long silence when he finished. Finally, his uncle spoke a few sentences.

"You know anything about San Roque?" Martin asked.

I told him what I had learned during my visit there with Masoir.

"You know their relationship to us?"

"No. But I know that pot you brought to me was from the Ma."

The old man looked at me and smiled.

Then Martin and his uncle each told me a story. The uncle's story was long and lyrical and from the ancient past. Martin's story was short, sad and from the recent past.

After listening to the stories, I understood everything I needed to know about all the pots, even my smashed copies. I figured out most of the details about the murder on the way back to Albuquerque, and those I didn't figure out, I made guesses about.

I parked in my usual spot in the alley, but instead of going in, I walked through the alley and circled around Miss Gladys' Gift Shop to the back of St. Neri and found Father Groaz in his study. After we exchanged greetings, I handed him the paper with the three letters on it.

"The police took this paper from the body of Master Gerstner?"

I nodded.

"Do they know what it means?"

"I doubt it."

"Do you?"

"Horace Arthur thinks it's the first three letters of my name. I haven't seen Gerstner in over twenty years, so the only reason for him to have my name on him would be if the person who killed him is trying to frame me, but you can't do that by typing out three letters, so I never took Arthur's idea seriously. I thought it was just the word 'hub'. I didn't know why he would have that word on him, but I didn't try to figure it out because it didn't seem related to the murder. Then I realized something about the letters—they're Cyrillic."

"So you *do* know what it means."

"No, but I think I know the sounds they make. See if I'm right. The Н makes the 'N' sound. The Ц makes the 'Ts' sound, and the 'В' makes the 'V' sound. So the word must be pronounced something like *nootsva*."

He roared with laughter and his belly shook like Saint Nick.

"I guess I didn't get it right."

"Actually, Youbird," he said while drying his eyes with a handkerchief, "you did vary well. That is precisely the sound such a word would make, but is not a word. These are initials. They stand for *Natzionalen Tsenter Vuzrazhdaneto*."

"That's easy for you to say." I was hoping to provoke another belly laugh, but all I got with that line was a chuckle.

"In English is something like 'National Center for Rebirth'. He wrote the words for me in the in Cyrillic—национален център възражданєто.

Then he told me more about the Rusyns and the НЦВ.

53

At four the next morning, I backed the Bronco onto the apron in front of the exit gate at Rio Grande Lofts, left the engine running and lowered the tailgate. The back was loaded with a sturdy steel bar and iron discs weighing fifty pounds each. Each disc had a hole in the middle. The bar was designed to go through the holes in the discs, but I didn't put it there. I used it to slide the discs under the gate and over next to the column that contained either a low field or a high field magnetic detection device. I didn't care which one because I was pretty certain I had purchased enough body building equipment to activate either style.

And sure enough, after I had pushed several hundred pounds of iron under the gate, it opened. I jumped in to the Bronco and backed through past the gate-opening device. The gate closed and I loaded all of the weights save one back in the truck. I pulled forward enough to make the gate re-open then got out and jammed a fifty-pound disk against it. With the gate thusly secured, I drove around the corner and parked two blocks away where I sat for a while recovering from the exertion.

I walked back to Rio Grande Lofts and removed the iron disc from the gate. As the gate closed, I carried the weight to the glassed in area where I discovered the keypad there had also been replaced by a card reader. It didn't matter. This was my seventh unauthorized visit to Rio Grande Lofts, and I knew it was my last, so I took a less meticulous approach to getting in. I thumped the weight against the glass panel next to the door and it shattered, making some noise but not enough to be heard outside the basement. The noise I was more concerned about was an alarm. When I didn't hear one, I set about doing what I had come to do.

I ducked through the frame where the glass had been and climbed the stairs to the second floor. Why the second floor? Because I didn't want to risk riding the elevator past the lobby in case some late reveler or early riser caused the elevator car to open there. And I went only as far as two because I had just unloaded and loaded several hundred pounds of iron in fifty pound increments, and I was too damned tired to climb any higher.

I tried the stairway door and it opened. As I suspected, my clay piece was still in place. The police had discovered the clay pieces on ten and eleven because they knew I had left the party on ten, and they suspected I had gone to eleven to kill Gerstner. The crime scene encompassed only those two floors. There was no need for them to check the lower doors, and they hadn't.

I took the elevator up, loided a lock and broke in to a loft.

I made as little noise and spent as little time as I could. Then I left with the door unlocked.

And rode the elevator to a different loft where I loided another lock, but this time to an apartment I knew was empty, so I was a lot more relaxed.

Then I rode back to the first loft, went through the door I had left unlocked, spent even less time inside and locked the door on my way out. During this entire adventure, I was wearing thin plastic gloves Sharice had given me from their supply at the dental office.

The scary part was behind me and there was a spring in my step as I opened the door to the stairwell and started down.

Then I heard quick noisy footsteps coming up. I leaned over the railing and saw two uniformed policemen several stories below. I started back towards the door then remembered the clay was gone from ten and eleven. My only hope was to get to nine before the cops did and hope that nine, like two, still had its clay plug.

I did and it did.

No one was roaming about on nine at that hour of the morning and the police were probably headed to ten and eleven, but when they didn't find me there, they would no doubt search the whole building. I assumed I had triggered a silent alarm when I broke the glass. Or maybe an early jogger had seen the broken glass. It didn't much matter why the police had arrived. They were here and the odds were I was the reason, so I had to get out.

But how? I didn't want to risk the stairway or the elevators because the police would be moving around searching, and that meant they could be using either or both. I could loid my way into an apartment and hope it was empty, but so what if it was? They'd probably search every apartment. If I could get down to four, maybe Stella would protect me. Or maybe not. What story would I give her to make her say no one was there when the police knocked on her door?

Then I heard the elevator door opening.

54

They had in fact gone to the eleventh floor and searched every apartment, upsetting a few residents in the process.

They had also posted men in the stairwell and each elevator and then started searching every apartment on each floor, working their way down from eleven. They also searched the first floor and the basement, looking in and under each car, but they didn't find anyone who wasn't supposed to be in the building.

Then they scratched their heads and went home.

At least that's what I think happened. I was in the building the entire time, but I wasn't an eyewitness to any of their searching except on the ninth floor.

Actually, I wasn't an *eye* witness there either, more of an *ear* witness.

I heard them knocking on doors, and I heard one resident say to another that this used to be a good building and now look, first we have a murder then we have cops running everywhere. The other resident said, "There must be drug dealers in here. Have you noticed they change the security system every time we turn around?"

I also noticed the cops were surprisingly efficient. They were on the ninth floor less than twenty minutes. I knew how long it took to search one of those apartments if all you wanted to look for was something large like a person because I had done it myself. Of course they may have been searching more than one floor at a time. I had no idea how many troops had been dispatched.

So I waited a very long time, and fortunately no one on the ninth floor chose to throw out any garbage that morning, so eventually I was able to climb out of my hiding place, walk down the stairs to the basement, walk through the glassed-in area, wait until the first person left that morning, and run through the exit gate behind her car. Who cared if she saw me and called the police? I was in the Bronco and on my way in less than a minute.

I entered Old Town and made a left on the south side of the Plaza. Then I made three right turns around the Plaza, and if you think that put me back where I started, you are good at spatial reasoning.

From there I drove back to Central, turned left and got to within four blocks of Susannah's apartment when I spotted a police cruiser just like the one I'd seen in front of my shop. The one near Tristan's apartment made it a hat trick.

I figured if they were that intent on finding me, they probably had an APB out, so I took the old bridge over to the west side, avoiding the freeway, and drove north on Corrales Road through Bernalillo and then the nine miles on the state highway to Martin Seepu's pueblo.

I parked out of sight and banged on his door. "Let me in," I said when he opened the door.

"The Indian way," he said, mocking my voice, "is to greet people with a salutation."

"How," I said.

"How?"

He let me in anyway, and I told him the police were after me. He told me he already knew about it from Channel 17's Roving Reporter.

"I was at my sister's house when the news came on. That Roving Reporter is good looking for a white woman. Anyway, she was in front of an apartment with crime scene tape on it, and she said a murder had taken place inside that apartment, and the police had arrested you but then let you go even though dozens of witnesses had placed you at the scene."

"Shoot. What else did she say?"

"Well, it was a longer piece than she usually does. She seemed really fired up about it, too. She said the victim was someone you had a long-standing grudge against and what else . . . Oh, that you had been at a party in the building, left the party, the partygoers heard a shot, and then you came back covered with blood."

"Covered with blood!"

"That's what she said."

I was pretty certain I was back to doing my own ironing.

"Then she closed the report by saying it was time for the police to take action, so I guess that's why they're after you."

"That and the fact I broke in to that apartment again early this morning."

He shook his head. "And white people think Indians are dumb."

"I need to use your phone."

"You know I don't have a phone. You want me to send up some smoke signals?"

"Martin, for the first time in my life, I wish I had a cell phone."

"My sister has a cell phone. You want me to get it?"

I used it to call Whit Fletcher. After he tried to talk me in to surrendering and then tried to remind me in oblique language that he and I had never been in Rio Grande Lofts together, I finally got him to listen. Then I explained everything to him, and he agreed to set up a meeting the next night at my shop.

55

"I hope you can pull this off, Hubert. My career may be riding on it."

"Have I ever let you down?"

He shrugged and brushed his hair off his forehead. "Thanks for covering for me when we ran in to that reporter."

"You knew who she was?"

"Everybody knows who she is. I guess I was sort of surprised the way she looked at you. You two got something going?"

"You surprised at that, Whit?"

"Tell the truth, Hubert, I always figured you for a fag, you being so old and never married."

"I hope you don't say things like that around other people."

"The detective course had an entire lesson devoted to manners and tact."

"I'm going to the back to gather my thoughts. You let me know when everyone is here."

The eventual crowd in my shop that evening included Walter Masoir, Martin Seepu, Frederick Blass, Horace Arthur, Bertha Zell, Jack Wiezga, Vlade Glastoc, Whit Fletcher, two uniformed policemen, Susannah, Tristan, Father Groaz, Layton Kent and one of his paralegals. I own four kitchen chairs, one reading chair, one stool, and two patio chairs, all of which had been pressed in to service in the front of the shop. That left six of us standing—Whit, the two uniforms, Susannah, Tristan and me.

"I should start by saying, 'You're probably wondering why I called you all together', but you probably already know why. I need to prove I didn't murder Ognan Gerstner."

I didn't add that the only way to do that was to prove who did.

Then I laid it all out. "The distinguished-looking gentleman to my far left is Professor Walter Masoir. A few weeks ago, he told me he believed Ognan Gerstner had kept a set of pots that were supposed to be sent back to the San Roque Pueblo. I decided to try to recover those pots and return them to their rightful owner."

Fletcher rolled his eyes and cleared his throat.

"As you all know if you watch the news, I was at a party the night Gerstner was killed. The party was at the residence of Frederick Blass who resides in the building where Gerstner lived. Mr. Blass is the gentleman in the black windbreaker seated at the back right. I admit I left the party and broke in to Gerstner's apartment. But I didn't murder him. I was looking for the pots when I was startled by a loud noise that I now realize was a gunshot. I was so startled, in fact, that I fell and incurred a scratch on my arm that bled slightly. When I returned to the party, Mr. Horace Arthur noticed the blood on my shirt. Mr. Arthur is here seated next to Mr. Blass. Incidentally, Mr. Arthur, the news reported that I was covered in blood. Is that what you told the police?"

"I told them there were a few drops on your arm. I can't say what the press reported, but they are lackeys of the police, so nothing would surprise me."

Given that Whit and his men were helping me, I didn't appreciate the political commentary, but I moved on. "Gerstner was later found shot to death in his apartment. Since the shot that killed him seemed to have been fired while I was in that very apartment, the police naturally assumed I had fired it. But I knew I hadn't fired it, and I knew Gerstner hadn't been in his apartment when it was fired. So despite the fact the police in this city do a great job, I knew they were wrong in this case."

"Cut the crap, Hubert, and get on with it," said Fletcher.

"The best explanation I could come up with at first was that Gerstner had been shot in another apartment while I was in his, and then later the murderer had placed Gerstner's body back in his own apartment. But why would the murderer move the body? I thought it was strangely coincidental that the shot was heard while I was in Gerstner's apartment. I know there's such a thing as bad luck, but this was almost too bad to be merely coincidence. So I tried to figure out if another explanation might be possible, and of course it is. There could have been two shots—the one everyone at the party heard and another one that actually killed Gerstner."

"How would that work?" asked Susannah as I had prompted her to do.

"Suppose someone had been thinking about killing Gerstner. Suppose further that the person saw I was away from the party and took the opportunity to fire a shot. Then later, that person kills Gerstner and puts the body in 1101, Gerstner's apartment, to frame me."

"That sounds rather far-fetched," said Blass.

"I agree. But the night of the party was not the first time I'd been in Gerstner's apartment."

"Every time he speaks," said Arthur in deadpan, "he admits another crime."

"I have discussed his situation with the authorities," said Layton, "and they have granted him immunity."

"Who are you?" asked Bertha.

"I, madam, am Layton Kent, attorney for Mr. Schuze."

"Another criminal profession," said Arthur.

I pressed on. "In my previous visit to Gerstner's apartment, I found one of the stolen pots, but I left it there because I wanted to recover all of them, not just one. While I was there, someone entered the apartment. I hid behind the couch and peeked under it, so all I saw were shoes. I left without being detected, so the person who came in doesn't know I was there. I went down to the parking garage in the basement and watched for an hour. No one wearing those shoes left the building, so I assume the person lived in the building."

"The person might have left through the lobby," said Bertha.

"True. But this is not a walking city. People who live in Rio Grande Lofts generally take their cars when they leave the building."

"Speculation," said Horace.

"Granted. But what is not speculation is that I saw those same shoes again."

"How can you be sure they were the same shoes?" asked Bertha.

"Because they were unique. And the feet I saw them on were the feet of Frederick Blass."

"Are you accusing me of breaking into Gerstner's apartment like you did?"

"Yes, and also of murder."

"Murder?" He smiled and looked around at the others. "This must be Hubert's idea of a bizarre parlor game. I admit to having a stunning collection of unique shoes, but that is hardly evidence for murder."

He was smooth, all right. "Unfortunately for you, there may be some stronger evidence. The police entered your apartment with a warrant moments after you left to come here. By now they probably have your dueling pistols at the crime lab. I'm confident one of them will turn out to be the murder weapon."

"Your confidence is unwarranted."

"The police will also be searching for any of the missing pots."

"Let them do so," he said with a shrug of his shoulders. "Mr. Kent," he said, "perhaps after this is over I can discuss with you the possibility of court action against Mr. Schuze for libel."

"Quite impossible," said Layton. "In the first place, Mr. Schuze is my client. Bringing an action against him would constitute a conflict. And secondly, no libel is committed when the charges are true."

"I'm no longer willing to participate in this farce," said Blass, and he rose to go.

"Sit down, Blass," said Fletcher.

"Am I under arrest?"

"Let's just say you're being detained for questioning. My men in your apartment will contact me when they've finished their work, and then we'll see if anyone needs arresting."

Blass sat back down and glared at Fletcher then at me. Even though he was a murderer, I felt guilty about proving it, and I looked away. No one said anything and the silence in the room was as thick as an adobe wall.

Then there was a knock on the door.

It was not the police. It was Miss Gladys Claiborne with a tray of desserts.

56

Fletcher looked at the door and rolled his eyes. "It's the same dame was here last time, Hubert. Tell her to go away."

I opened the door and explained it was not a social gathering.

"Well, I can see that," she said, pushing me aside with the tray and heading for the counter. "That same nice detective is here again, but I think these young men in uniform are different ones. What are their names, detective?"

"Ma'am, this here's an official police matter. I'm going to have to ask you to leave."

"Oh, come on detective, we might as well eat while we're waiting for your men to report," said Horace Arthur.

"We don't need—" started Whit.

"I agree with Horace," said Bertha, interrupting him. "I, for one, am famished."

"Me, too, Whit," chimed in Susannah.

The two uniforms had already walked over to the counter and were examining the offerings.

Whit threw up his hands.

Miss Gladys proudly peeled the plastic wrap off the tray. "Detective, you look like a strong man. Would you be so kind as to slant this tray up while I explain what's on it?"

Whit walked resignedly behind the counter and lifted the tray to a perfect angle for display.

There was strawberry pie. Miss Gladys didn't give out recipes. I guess she didn't think it appropriate for an official police matter, but I knew what was in it because she had made it for me before. It's a ready-made graham cracker crust from the baking aisle, two packages of frozen strawberries, strawberry Jell-O and a can of ReadyWhip. The names of Miss Gladys' ingredients are frequently followed by ™. I would tell you how to put everything together, but you can probably figure it out yourself.

There were also marshmallow brownies, praline pie and something called 7-Up cake.

The praline pie is a normal pecan pie with the Karo syrup caramelized before the pecans are added. Everyone grabbed something, even Frederick Blass who evidently thought he had nothing to fear. He was talking to Jack Wiezga and eating a marshmallow brownie.

Fletcher gave in and started in on a slice of 7-Up cake. "Hubert, you got any coffee?"

I retrieved my coffeemaker from under the counter. While I was starting the process, I heard Miss Gladys ask Whit if he was married. He looked at her warily and said he was. She seemed disappointed, but recovered swiftly with an offer for him to take some dessert home to his wife. He allowed as how the 7-Up cake was the best cake he'd ever eaten. "Nice and moist," he said, "not like my wife's cakes. You need a glass of water handy just to swallow."

The coffee finished brewing, but the phone rang and everyone was spared having to drink it.

I answered and passed the phone to Fletcher who listened, muttered a few yeahs and hmms and then hung up. "That was one of my buddies back at the station. They found one of them pots hidden in your closet, Blass, and they found blood on one of them old pistols, too. Of course we had a sample of Gerstner's blood from the crime scene, and the blood on your pistol matched perfectly. I guess instead of hiring Mr. Kent here for a libel suit, you might want to ask him if he would defend you against a murder charge."

Blass started to say something, then thought better of it and remained silent while Fletcher read him his rights

Miss Gladys said, "Oh, my."

57

"Wow, Uncle Hubert. You're going to be a hero when you return those pots to San Roque. You are going to return them, right?"

"All the originals."

Tristan had helped me carry the chairs back where they belonged, and he was now ensconced in one of them, tilting it back on its two rear legs and drinking a bottle of beer. I'd offered him a glass for the beer, but as usual he'd declined.

"I like that music," he said.

"It's Lionel Hampton."

"What is it, like the 1920s?"

"More like the forties."

"But even that's before you were born, so how did you come to like it?"

"The Beatles were before you were born, but you like them."

"Good point. But all their stuff has been digitally remastered. I don't think there'd be enough market to justify that for this Hampton guy." He was walking to the refrigerator as he talked.

"Probably not," I agreed. "On the other hand, most people who listen to Lionel Hampton wouldn't know what digitally re-mastered means. They still think vinyl creates the highest fidelity."

"You're kidding me. That's really an old 33 1/3 disc? Where's the turntable?"

"It's not a record. It's satellite radio."

"You have any salsa to go with . . ." He brought his head out of the fridge. "Satellite radio? The one I brought over for you? You told me you'd never use it."

"Well, I didn't think I'd be able to. I mean, there's not even a knob to tune in stations."

"Uncle Hubert, when's the last time you saw a radio with a twist tuner?"

"Is that a knob?"

"Yep."

"The radio in my Bronco has one."

"Your Bronco is older than I am. See, no matter how good your ear and how dexterous you might be with your fingers, you can't get a twist tuner to center on a signal. A digital tuner measures the frequency and the amplitude of the station's signal and—"

"Tristan?"

"Yeah?"

"I think I have some salsa in the cabinet." I found a jar, opened it and poured it in a bowl.

Tristan opened a bag of tortilla chips. "Did you figure out why those guys smashed your pots?"

"I didn't, but Martin told me what probably happened. As you know, San Roque has little interaction with the outside world. Occasionally a young person leaves and doesn't return. A few of them are here in the city, but they often don't fare well. A small band of them are on drugs. Martin thinks they remembered a tribal story about treasure in pots, so they broke mine open hoping to find a treasure."

"Which they obviously didn't find, but why take the pieces?"

"I guess they wanted to break them in to smaller pieces to see what they could find. The process was taking too long, so they took the pieces somewhere where they could examine them without worrying about the police showing up."

"Maybe they thought the treasure was weed, and they planned to grind up the pots and smoke them."

That brought a laugh from both of us.

"Oh," he said, "I have Stella Ramsey doing the news if you want to see it."

"You know I don't have a television, much less a videotape player."

He laughed again. "Videotape players are so yesterday. I have it right here on my Blackberry."

And he powered it up and there was Stella. Even on a very small screen, she was beautiful.

"Thanks for including me tonight," he said after the show was over. "It was radical."

Before he left, I asked him how he was doing, but you already know how that goes.

58

Order was restored to my little corner of the cosmos the next day at five, a margarita in my hand, Susannah across the table.

"I still don't get how you knew Frederick fired that shot while you were burgling Gerstner's apartment."

"The shoes were the key."

"When did you see those shoes on him again?"

"I didn't. That was a lie I told because the truth was too complicated to explain at the gathering last night. But I saw him in some other exotic footwear, and it made me wonder if he was the one I saw from under the couch."

"But you said that was a woman. Your even heard her putting the seat down."

"I thought it was a woman because I've never seen shoes like that on a man. Once I had it in my mind it was a woman, then of course I thought the clack was her putting the toilet seat down."

"Because you were in a man's apartment, and you pigs always leave the seat up."

I chose not to argue that point. "When I started wondering if it was Blass, I realized the same sound is made by putting the seat *up*. Once I started thinking about him, the reasons to think he did it kept piling up."

"Like?"

"First, he had the opportunity to fire the shot."

"So did everyone else at the party."

"In theory, yes. But if it were one of the guests, that would mean he anticipated that I would be there and would sneak during the evening, so he brought a gun along to fire out the window while I was gone."

"Not very likely."

"Right. The only person in a position to seize the opportunity of my sneaking out would be the host. First, he wouldn't have to bring a gun to the party. He already had one there. Second, he could move around more easily than a guest. He could go in to the second bedroom, lock the door and fire one of the dueling pistols out the window. A guest would have to wander around in an unfamiliar apartment, find the pistol, figure out how to fire it, etc. No, if anyone fired a pistol, it had to be Blass. And remember, after I saw the shoes from under the couch, no one left the building with those shoes on. And the night of the party, the Ma pot was gone from Gerstner's apartment, so I figured the person with the fancy shoes took the pot and lived in the building."

"But that's not conclusive."

"Conclusive? It's not even very plausible. But it was the only theory I had. Once I started thinking about how that theory might work, things started falling in line, things that were a lot more plausible and even conclusive."

"Such as?"

"I knew Gerstner had the pots, and I figured he must have been selling them off to supplement his retirement checks. But Gerstner didn't seem the type to be able to pull that off. He would have needed a high-class fence."

"Enter Frederick Blass?"

"Exactly. And then I remembered Jack Wiezga called Blass a fence, and that started me thinking about Blass' apartment. You remember how fancy it is?"

"Probably better than you do," she said while looking down at the floor.

"He has paintings by Degas, Gorman and other expensive original art. Department heads make a decent salary, but he had to be living well above his means."

"Remember I told you he talked a lot about money?"

I nodded.

"What else?" she asked.

"When I went to Rio Grande Lofts with Fletcher, I found the first piece of real evidence—Gerstner's check book. On the part where you list the checks, there were two with Blass' name."

"But couldn't those checks have been unrelated to the pots? Maybe he won money from Frederick in a poker game. And I don't understand how you knew someone tried to frame you in the first place. Maybe that shot we heard was just a car backfiring, and later that night Gerstner came home and someone killed him."

"I thought that at first, too, remember? But when I saw the murder scene, there was very little blood on the couch. I asked Whit about it, and he said the murderer must have tried to wipe it off. But why would the murderer try to wipe off the blood? I mean, he left the body there, so it was obvious there had been a murder. On top of that, everyone knows some of the blood would remain no matter how much you tried to clean it up. It just didn't make sense. Then I thought of Ptolemy and Kepler."

"Oh, brother—not that again."

"Sorry. It's how my brain works. Ptolemy and Kepler gave two explanations for the same thing. I realized there were two explanations for the blood being swirled around on the couch. One was what Whit told me—someone tried to wipe it off. The second explanation is that someone tried to wipe it *on*. Once I thought of that, I realized it made more sense. The murderer must have shot Gerstner somewhere else and brought the body to Gerstner's apartment. Then he tried to make it look like the shooting had taken place there by smearing Gerstner's blood on the couch. Now, there's no reason to risk moving the body and wiping blood on the couch unless you're trying to frame someone. So the blood on the couch was the final piece of the puzzle from my perspective. Once I realized the murderer was trying for a frame, everything came together."

"But why frame you?"

"Well, that part was just bad luck. Blass knew who I was and he knew the story about Gerstner expelling me. Blass also has a facile mind. When he saw me leave the party, it must have occurred to him that he might be able to frame me, so he fired a shot outside the window just in case. If he didn't go ahead and kill Gerstner later, what had he lost? A little gunpowder, maybe a small ball of lead. Obviously, he was already thinking about killing Gerstner, and this gave him a way to make it safer to do so. I also talked to Whit about that shot. Guess what he told me?"

"What?"

"Those dueling pistols use old fashioned black powder, and they're much louder than a modern pistol."

"So that's why it was so loud."

I nodded. "Now here's where Blass got really lucky. Of course he couldn't have known where I was going when I stepped outside. Maybe he thought I went out for a smoke. That's what I told Horace Arthur when I came back in, and that's also what I told Whit Fletcher. But it didn't matter for Blass' purpose. People saw me leave, so they would know I wasn't there. All that mattered was that I was somewhere else. But the somewhere else happened to be Gerstner's apartment, which is naturally where Blass dumped the body."

You could almost see the little light bulb hovering over Susannah's head. "Because when they found the body, it had to be somewhere you could have gone during the short time you were away from the party."

"Exactly. If Blass had dumped the body up in Tijeras canyon, my being at the party would have given me an alibi instead of incriminating me."

"So he had to put Gerstner's body in the building, and the best place was Gerstner's own apartment. And the lucky part for Blass is that was exactly where you'd been. Do you think anyone heard the second shot, the one that actually killed Gerstner? Or did Blass challenge Gerstner to a duel somewhere out in the desert?"

We both laughed at that and took another drink.

"I'm sure the shot we heard was from one of the dueling pistols, but the murder weapon was not one of those pistols. You know I don't know anything about guns, but I imagine a dueling pistol wouldn't be a murderer's choice of weapon. They only fire one shot and even that's not very reliable. No, he used a modern dependable weapon, a Kel-Tec .380 to be exact."

"How do you know that?"

"Whit told me. They found it in his car. And typical of Blass, it was the chrome-plated model. The ballistic test matched perfectly with the slug they took out of Gerstner's head."

"But what about the blood on the dueling pistol?"

There was no reason I could think of not to tell her. "I put it there."

"No!"

"Yes. On my last trip to Rio Grande Lofts, I broke in to Blass' loft and got one of the dueling pistols. Then I went upstairs and broke in to Gerstner's loft. I rubbed some damp toilet paper against the couch then against the muzzle of the gun. Then I took the gun and put it back. For good measure, I hid that copy of a Ma pot I made in Blass' second bedroom closet."

"You framed him!"

"I did. He framed me, then I framed him. The big difference, of course, is that he actually did it." Then I thought about it. "Maybe I didn't frame him. Can you frame someone who's already guilty?"

"I still can't believe he is guilty. I know you proved it, and now I know they even found the gun he used. But why did he do it, Hubie?"

"Well, this is just guesswork. The Ma were missing eighteen pots. If we assume Gerstner started out with all eighteen, then fifteen had already been sold since I recovered only three. I told you there were only two deposit slips with Blass' name on them. So the way I see it, Blass sold fifteen pots but had only paid Gerstner for two of them so far. So Blass owed Gerstner for thirteen pots. I estimate those pots to be worth about fifty thousand each, so Blass owed Gerstner $650,000."

She shook her head in dismay. "He doesn't seem like such a bad person."

"I agree. I told you how much I liked him after the party. I think he just got in so far over his head that he couldn't see any other way out. Maybe Gerstner grew tired of waiting and threatened to go to the police if Blass didn't pay up."

"But wouldn't Blass have gotten some of the money for being the fence?"

"Of course. Blass' share could have been ten percent. Or say it was even a fifty-fifty deal. That's still a third of a million he owed Gerstner. Knowing how he lived, he may already have spent it."

"So the Rusyn connection had nothing to do with it?"

"No, that turned out to be a dead end. But it did explain why Gerstner had that piece of paper with the first three letters of my name on it."

She gave me a quizzical look.

"Actually, your paper on Nesterov's painting of the Tsarevich Dimitri was what did it."

"Huh?"

"The letters on Gerstner's piece of paper were Cyrillic. What looks like an 'H' is actually an 'N'. Or at least that's the sound it makes. The 'U' thing makes that 'Ts' sound."

"Or that 'Cz' sound," she added with a crooked smile.

"Right. And the 'B' actually makes the 'V' sound. So what looked like HUB is actually the Cyrillic equivalent of NTV."

"Which is what, national television?"

"No, but they are initials."

I handed her the paper on which Father Groaz had written: национален център възражданєто

She stared at it for a minute then said, "Natzeonalen tsenter vuzrazhdaneto?"

"Wow, your pronunciation sounds exactly like the way Father Groaz said it. I'm impressed you can read Cyrillic."

"I can't really read it. I know the actual meanings of only a few dozen words. But doing the research on Nesterov had me seeing so much Cyrillic that I decided to memorize the sounds the letters make."

"That sounds like something I would do and you would criticize me for."

"Yeah, that's what I thought as I was doing it. You're a bad influence on me. Anyway, there are 30 letters and most of them appear in Nesterov's three names and the titles of his paintings, so by the time I'd finished the paper, I already knew most of the sounds. I'm guessing the first two words are 'national center'?"

"Right, and the last one means 'rebirth' or 'renaissance'."

"So what is it, an arts group of some sort?"

"Hardly. It's a band of fervent Rusyn nationalists. Evidently, they chose the term 'renaissance' because they admired a movement in neighboring Bulgaria that used that phrase. The Bulgarians were under Ottoman rule for five hundred years, and sometime in the eighteenth century they began to assert their national identity which eventually led to their liberation."

I could see she wasn't interested in Bulgarian history, so I didn't add the rest of the story Father Groaz had told me.

She stared back down at the paper and said, "Wouldn't it be a lot easier if they used the same alphabet as everyone else?"

"Probably. And it would reinforce your theory about country names that start with vowels."

"Right, because the U thing turns out not to be a vowel."

"So I guess that's not the first letter of Ukraine."

"I told you that already. The first letter of Ukraine is a 'T'—The Ukraine."

I chuckled and decided not to contest the point. "One of the things I found in Gerstner's filing cabinet was a copy of a letter he sent to the Ukrainian Embassy in Washington. It wasn't written in Cyrillic, but the wording was so indirect, it may as well have been. I think what it amounted to was an offer to sell them information about Rusyn activities. I don't know if they ever responded."

"So he really was a mole?"

"More of a rat I'd say."

We sat there for a while listening to the background noise of customers ordering tamales and the bartender mixing drinks.

Susannah said, "You remember that Maltese falcon? It looked like a big ugly tchotchke your grandmother might have had in her bookcase. But when they scraped the paint off it, it was encrusted with jewels. Are the pots like that?"

"Indeed they are. Except they have gold in them rather than jewels."

"You didn't put gold in the copy you made, did you?"

I shook my head.

"What will happen to that copy?"

"Right now it's evidence, but I doubt it will ever see the inside of a courtroom. Blass will probably plea-bargain."

"Why do you say that?"

"Because he knows he can't win at trial, and he has something to bargain with—the Ma pots. He can tell the police who he sold them to, and most of them will probably be recovered. That's important for the Ma, and I think the DA will know that. And Whit told me he also guesses Blass will bargain."

"So what will happen to him?"

"Fletcher or Blass?"

"Both."

"Blass will probably get a ten year sentence and serve about half of it."

"That doesn't seem like much for killing someone."

"Yeah. But the justice system is strange, Suze. Did you know that in the penalty phase of a murder trial, they can have witnesses testify about the victim, what a nice person he was, how much he could have done for society if he hadn't been killed, and things like that?"

"Well, I don't think anyone would say things like that about Gerstner."

"That's why the sentence may not be so long."

"That's awful, Hubie. It's like saying it's worse to kill a good person than a bad person."

"It doesn't seem right, does it? But that's the way it works. And so far as I know, Gerstner has no family, so no one will protest the light sentence. And then they have to give Blass a break for cooperating, so that's why I'm guessing ten years."

"What about Fletcher?"

"He gets to keep the Ma copy I made."

"How much is it worth?"

"I would probably ask five thousand for it in my replica shop."

"Why should that crooked cop get all that money?"

"I know it's galling, but he did help me clear myself."

"What about you? Will you get anything out of it?"

"Well, I avoid going to jail for murder, and who can put a price tag on that? I'll return the two originals to the Ma. But I'm keeping the genuine Ma copy. And unlike the copy I made, it's worth fifty grand because it's a genuine copy."

"A genuine copy?"

"That does sound odd, but you know what I mean—it doesn't have any gold in it."

"So you came out okay?"

"It looks like it. If I can sell the pot, I'll keep the money in reserve in case Consuela needs a transplant. She's eligible for some funding for indigent patients, and the fifty should cover what the government doesn't. And with all the publicity, maybe business will pick up. I'm ready to start turning out fakes again."

"Replicas, Hubie."

"Right." I rotated my glass and sipped my margarita. "You know what the worst part of this fiasco was?"

"What?"

"It was being five six and one forty and going in to that sporting goods store and buying all those weights. The whole staff looked at me like I was some kind of nut who thought lifting weights would turn me into Arnold what's-his-name."

"Schwarzenegger."

"Easy for you to say."

"This is all so amazing."

"I'm just glad it's over. You know how you always kid me about being a burglar? Well, I guess I sort of was one there for a while, but I am definitely not cut out for it. I was terrified going in to Blass' place with him asleep in it."

She had a sheepish look on her face. "He wasn't there, Hubie."

"He wasn't?"

"No."

"Where was he?"

She looked down at her empty margarita glass.

"Oh," I said.

I ordered another round for both of us, and after Angie brought them and went back to the bar, I said, "I'm sorry, Suze. Here I've been discussing Blass the murderer and not even thinking about how you must feel. I am like Spock sometimes, I know that. And I feel even worse because if I hadn't suggested that paragraph for your computer dating thing, he wouldn't have answered it, and you never would have dated him."

She looked up with tears in her eyes, but she brushed them away and gave me a really big smile.

"Hey, it's just another addition to the losers list: the married guy, the third grade vocabulary guy, the Pine-Sol aftershave guy and now the murderer guy."

"I must say you're taking it very well."

"I had concerns about him all along, but I swept them under the carpet. He was handsome and exciting, so why look a gift horse in the mouth?"

"That's what the Trojans said."

"He was too slick. I'm a rancher girl, Hubie. I don't need glitz. I just want someone honest and fun and, well, if he's good-looking, that would be all right. Is that too much to ask?"

I shook my head.

She pulled a piece of paper out of her purse. "Let me read you this message I got from the dating site this afternoon. The guy's name is Bob. That's a nice solid name, don't you think? Here's what he wrote. He said . . ."

You really can't keep a good woman down.

59

I had to skip Dos Hermanas the next day because I was having cocktails with the Masoirs.

Channel 17 must have felt guilty about how their Roving Reporter had sensationalized the story because their follow-up played up the angle that I was trying to help San Roque recover their pots.

Mrs. Masoir placed brie and water crackers on the coffee table and Professor Masoir mixed a pitcher of gin martinis. I don't like brie and I really don't like gin, but I like both the Masoirs, so I nibbled and sipped with them.

The professor asked me what would happen to the pots.

"I have three of them, two from the original set and one from the copy set."

"My God," he said. "I know you're an expert on pots, but how can you tell the originals from the copies? You'd never even seen a Ma pot before."

I place my martini on the coffee table, happy to talk for a while without sipping. "I owe it all to you for taking me to San Roque. If you hadn't got me in there, I never would have heard about melting stone."

"So you figured out what it is?"

"Yes. It's gold."

"Gold! They mixed gold dust with their clay?"

"No. They placed large discs of pure gold in the bottom of the pots. They only did that for their ceremonial pots, of course. The idea was to demonstrate their devotion to a certain goddess. I noticed how thick the pot bases were the first time I saw one, but I didn't think there was anything in there other than clay."

"Fascinating. How did you discover the thickness was from a disk of gold? Did Martin's uncle tell you?"

"Yes," I said, which was true. But I had figured it out before Martin's uncle told me. I didn't tell Professor Masoir I'd figured it out because I had done so while watching the inventory tag melt in the fire, and I didn't want to explain why I was burning an inventory tag.

"If the gold is sealed inside, how can you know it's there?"

"I had them x-rayed."

"Using modern magic to examine ancient magic," he said and shook his head. "So what happens to the two with gold in them?"

"I'd like you to take them back to San Roque."

"Isn't that nice, Walter? I told you he's such a nice young man."

"Yes, Mildred, you did and he is. He's also very generous. How much is that gold worth?"

"Looking at the x-rays, I'd estimate each pot contains a hundred cubic centimeters. I don't know the price of gold."

"I don't know the exact figure, but it's around $1000 an

ounce. That would be," he did a quick mental calculation, "in the neighborhood of twenty thousand dollars."

"Not a bad neighborhood, but you wouldn't want to break open the pot for the gold. I'm sure a collector would pay at least fifty thousand each for them."

"So you're giving up over a hundred thousand by returning the two originals."

"They're worth a lot more than that to the Ma. And besides, they don't belong to me."

A slight smile formed on his face. "I understand you don't always take that attitude about old pots."

"Walter!" said Mrs. Masoir.

"It's okay," I said to her. "He's right, but that's because the ancient pots I dig up have no clear link to today's Indians. The Ma pots were never in the ground."

"Does the pot the police found in Blass' apartment contain gold, or is it one of the Ma's copies?"

"Neither. It's one of my copies."

"Ah. And the one you have that's a real copy—strange phrase, but you know what I mean?"

"You said they didn't care about those, just the originals which I'm giving back, so I plan to keep the copy unless you advise me to the contrary."

"I'm certain the Ma will be happy for you to keep the copy. What about all the ones that are missing?"

"Gerstner sold them. Or rather, Blass sold them for Gerstner. I think Blass will cooperate in recovering them to lessen his sentence and the police will be able to track down the pots and get them."

"So when I return the two to the Ma, I can tell them others may be forthcoming?"

"Yes, if they're originals. If they're copies, I'd like to keep them."

"So tell me, Hubert, one anthropologist to another, what was the story behind the pots?"

I told him the story came from Martin's pueblo and had been told to me by Martin's uncle with Martin translating. My English version probably didn't do the story justice from a poetic perspective, but it was all I had to offer.

"The rain god mated with the river goddess and a set of twins resulted from their union. They were beautiful children and she named them Left and Right, but the rain god's wife, who was the mountain goddess, was jealous, so she stole the twins and buried them in the mountain. Those are the two peaks visible to the north of the pueblo, the ones they call left peak and right peak. The mountain goddess also made the rain god promise to withhold rain from the land through which the river flows, and the river dried up and the land became a desert. When the river goddess discovered her twins were gone, she began to weep, and her tears eroded the soil off the mountains, releasing the twins. They went down to the river and each one started a tribe. Left did not honor his mother, and for half the year she thinks about him and weeps and the river flows. Right did honor his mother, and she thinks about him for the other half of the year and the river dries up."

"Let me guess," said Masoir. "The way in which Right and his tribe honor his mother is to seal up gold in their pots to symbolize the twins in the mountains."

I nodded.

"And Martin's pueblo is Left and San Roque is Right."

I nodded again.

We sat in silence for several minutes. Masoir seemed to be reflecting on what I'd told him. Finally he turned to me and said, "I am indebted to you, Hubert. For the first time since I left the University, I'm excited about my discipline again. I thought all that was behind me, but the trip to San Roque and the saga of the pots have reminded me of why I took up anthropology all those many years ago as a young man. Think about that story. Twins are a recurrent theme from Cain and Abel to Romulus and Remus, and of course the use of two hills or peaks to symbolize the female and fertility is found in every human myth. I could go on," he laughed, "but I fear I would break into a lecture."

"When you came to my shop earlier this month, you asked me what big ideas I learned in anthropology."

"As I recall, you didn't answer that question," he said with a gleam in his eye.

"Well, I'm prepared to answer it now. The most important lesson I learned is that all people in all places at all times are basically the same. In the million years since we started speaking and using tools, we humans have developed thousands of cultures, but the ways in which they are alike are fundamental, and the ways in which they are different are only superficial."

"Well put! And were it not true, there would be no science of anthropology because no culture would ever have enough in common with another to study and understand it. Of course our insights about other cultures are perhaps never completely accurate, but we might say the same of our own culture. Indeed, the longer I live, the less I seem to understand my own culture."

I knew exactly how he felt.

He shook his head in wonderment. "I sought assistance from you by explaining what the situation was and what I hoped you would do, and Martin's uncle sought assistance in the same endeavor by simply putting a pot in your hands. Theirs is an amazing culture."

"It is. I was a volunteer teacher at their pueblo many years ago as an idealistic undergraduate. I asked one of the kids to draw a horse. He started by drawing four ovals on the paper. Those were the hooves. Then he drew the rest of the horse. It wasn't drawn any better than you would expect from any grade school kid anywhere, but the hooves were exactly where they should be when a horse is standing. So I asked him to draw a running horse, and he drew four more ovals. When he completed that horse, it looked like it was running."

"Remarkable."

"I thought so. Incidentally, that little boy's name was Martin Seepu."

60

When I got back home from the Masoirs, it was a cold and crisp high desert night and the stars were beckoning.

I aimed my refractor at Jupiter, a popular target for amateur astronomers because it's two-and-a-half times larger than all the other planets combined and therefore easy to see. It's also got a lot to look at with its many moons, colorful alternating bands and famous red spot. The spot is actually a storm, somewhat like a hurricane on Earth, except ours are atmospheric hiccups by comparison. Jupiter's storm is three times larger than the earth and has been swirling around for at least four hundred years!

But I wasn't thinking about Jupiter as much as I was about Stella. When Tristan had shown me her newscast, it started with her theme song, Jupiter, from Holtz' famous work, *The Planets*. Holtz subtitled Jupiter "the bringer of jollity." But I was feeling pangs of longing.

I don't like most classical music, but Jupiter is the best of Holtz' eight themes. Why only eight? Because the ninth planet hadn't been discovered when Holtz wrote *The Planets*. Pluto was first sighted in 1929 by Clyde Tombaugh who, rather ironically it seemed to me at that moment, taught astronomy right here in New Mexico. He is also credited with determining the vortex nature of Jupiter's Great Red Spot which I was gazing at.

Professional astronomers call Jupiter a failed star. If it had been a little larger at the birth of the solar system, it would have become a second sun in our solar system. Jupiter could have been a star. Stella and I could have been . . . What?

I saw a shadow on Jupiter's surface and, after a little work, managed to focus in on Io, the moon that was casting that shadow. I felt that was an omen because you rarely get a good look at Io unless it's against a background of black sky above Jupiter's equator. Galileo was the first person to spot it, and that was 400 years ago using a very crude telescope by today's standards.

The name is from Greek mythology. Like most stories from Greek mythology, the tale of Io combines a few observations about human nature with a very confusing plot line I can never remember. The part I did remember was that Zeus fell in love with Io. Hera, Mrs. Zeus, was jealous and gave Io to Argus, the guy with a hundred eyes. I guess that's why a brand of cameras was named after him. Io later set Prometheus free, or maybe she chained him up—I don't remember. But it got her condemned to wander forever.

Io is solid like earth and has plains, volcanoes and an atmosphere. The atmosphere is mostly sulfur dioxide. Volcanic soil is good for growing grapes and sulfur dioxide is used in winemaking, but the temperature on Io is a bit frigid for viticulture. It's only a third the size of Earth, so it doesn't have much gravity, but it does have some, sort of like our moon. I remembered those spectacular pictures from our moon looking back at Earth, and I tried to imagine what it would be like to be on Io looking down at the swirling mass of gas that is Jupiter. You'd be able to see huge lightning bolts and extensive auroras. I wondered if you could hear the Jovian winds. They blow at over 500 miles per hour.

And after a while I realized it had happened. My concerns had drifted away, leaving me to contemplate a pleasurable ignorance. If I lived as long as Io, I would still never understand the universe. We can find the things that are out there, and we can measure and track them, but we can never really understand. Without realizing it, I had stopped thinking about Stella.

The heavens are awesome and addictive. Clyde Tombaugh was one of the addicts. He made his first telescope as a boy using discarded farm machinery parts and a drive shaft from his father's 1910 Buick. Sixty-five years later, the Smithsonian Institute asked if it could have that first telescope for its museum. Clyde told them, "I'm still using it." He lived to be ninety and was fond of saying, "I've had a tour of the heavens."

He didn't know how prophetic those words would be. NASA launched a space probe to Pluto in 2006. The distance to that farthest planet is so great, it will take the probe until 2015 to arrive even though it is traveling at 50,000 miles per hour!

And nestled in among the various scientific instruments is a small metal container with the ashes of Clyde Tombaugh.

61

"Sorry I couldn't make it yesterday, Suze. I enjoyed visiting with the Masoirs, but I really missed our daily chat and our margaritas."

"What did they serve you?"

"A gin martini."

"Yuk!"

Angie brought the first round with the chips and salsa, and we settled in.

"I've been thinking about what you said about Ptolemy and Kepler," Susannah announced.

The chip I was about to dredge through the salsa broke off between my fingers.

"Don't look so startled."

"Sorry. It's just that you usually—"

"I think you got it wrong," she stated flatly.

"Got what wrong?"

"When you were explaining about the blood on the couch, you said the breakthrough was when you realized it made more sense to think the murderer wiped the blood *on* than it did to assume he tried to wipe it *off*."

"But that does make more sense."

"I agree. What doesn't make sense is comparing it to Ptolemy and Kepler giving two explanations for the same thing because Ptolemy's explanation is wrong. Earth is not the center of the universe, and planets don't travel in circles."

I stared at her. I couldn't believe she was initiating a discussion of this topic.

"Well?" she asked.

"Ptolemy did not get it wrong."

"Come on, Hubert. You don't believe the earth is the center of the universe."

"The center of something is a point equidistant from that thing's perimeter."

"Like Willard," she said proudly.

"Willard?"

"Yes. My hometown is the geographic center of New Mexico."

"I didn't know that." I pictured a map of the State and realized she was probably right. Willard doesn't have many claims to fame—they can't even claim Susannah since she actually grew up on a ranch twelve miles south-southwest of Willard.

"Anyway," I continued, "the universe, unlike New Mexico, has no perimeter. It's infinite. Therefore it has no center."

She mulled that over while she chewed on a chip. "Okay, but the planets don't travel in circles."

It was my turn to think for a while. "The goal of Ptolemy was to explain the motion of the planets. His system does that just as well as Kepler's. The only reason we think Kepler's system is better is because it's simpler."

"But if you were way out in outer space, outside our solar system and looking at it, you'd see the planets traveling in ellipses, not twirling around in circles around circles," she said.

"You might see them doing figure eights. Viewed from earth, the planets look like they reverse themselves. What you see is a function of where you are."

"And how many margaritas you've had," she said. I guessed that meant she was tired of astronomy talk because the next things she said was, "I met Bob today for a cup of coffee."

"I trust he didn't turn out to be someone you already knew."

"No, thank God. He turned out to be a normal, nice guy with a great sense of humor."

"How so?"

"When we were discussing how we would recognize each other, he asked me for a suggestion and I said, 'You could wear a monocle', and he laughed. We settled on him wearing a checked shirt, but when I showed up, he actually had a monocle. Anyway, we have our first date tonight."

"So you're having a good day."

"You, too. The paper made you out to be a hero."

"Yeah, but I know I'm not because—"

"I know, I know—you lack the iron will and steel nerves the job requires."

"You've heard me say that, huh?"

"Several times. But heroes don't need iron wills or steel nerves. All they need to do is the right thing, and you did that, Hubie. You returned those pots to the Ma."

"But there's something else bothering me."

"What's that?"

"I wonder if Gerstner's idea of selling the pots for profit came from me."

"That's ridiculous."

"You really think so?"

"Of course. The pots he threw you out for selling were ones you dug up by yourself. You never lied about that. Gerstner said he was returning the pots and then didn't. It's not the same thing at all."

"I guess you're right. Thanks, Suze."

"Hubie, don't look now, but a reporter has just roved in to Dos Hermanas."

I suppose the picture on the bus was professionally done and touched up to make her look her best, but she looked even better in person. Her hair and makeup were flawless, her skirt flared, and her taupe sweater fitted in such a way as to remind any good anthropologist of the myth of the twin peaks.

"Hi, Hubert. I wouldn't blame you if you said no, but could we talk for a moment?"

I told her we could, and I got up and pulled back a chair for her to sit in. "Could we talk in private?"

Susannah started to get up, but I said, "Anything I hear, Susannah can hear."

Stella remained standing. "Hubert, I'm really sorry about that report I did on you. I don't think it was unethical reporting because it was accurate in light of what we knew at the time, but I have to admit I took pleasure in doing it because I found out you lied to me, and I thought I was getting back at you. A professional journalist should always keep her personal feelings out of her stories."

The speech seemed practiced, but I appreciated it anyway. "It's big of you to admit that, Stella, and I want you to know I don't have any hard feelings about it. You were just doing your job."

For the first time since I had seen her in the elevator, she seemed nervous. She looked down at Susannah then back at me. "I'm really happy to hear you say that, Hubert." She hesitated for a moment and took a deep breath. "Could I buy you dinner tonight as a better way of saying I'm sorry?"

"I don't think so."

"Oh."

"In fact, I think it's better if we don't see each other again." I had a knot in my stomach after I said it.

There was the slightest intake of breath, but Stella held her composure like a pro. Then she kissed me on the cheek, said goodbye to Susannah and left.

I sat down and we watched her go. We both took a drink. Then we just sat there for a moment until Susannah said, "Why did you do that, Hubie?"

"Because I don't think it would work out in the long run. She's beautiful and sexy. If I keep seeing her, I'll just get hooked more deeply and it will become even harder to get out, and I'll end up miserable. It's like I've sampled some exotic drug, and the feeling was wonderful, but I need to stop before I become an addict."

"I think that's sort of how I felt about Blass. He was too handsome, too suave, and somehow I knew he wasn't the one for me, but I didn't have the good sense to act on my intuition."

"Well, even though I liked him after the party, I was suspicious of him even before I knew it was him when you read me what he wrote on the dating site and he used that hackneyed phrase, 'a cruel twist of fate'."

"And this from a man who called Gerstner a cancelled Czech?"

277

I just shrugged.

She eased into her mischievous smile. "I guess I was suspicious of Stella all along, too. She ran in to you by accident in that elevator, and you know what she turned out to be?"

I thought about it halfheartedly and then said, "I give up. What did she turn out to be?"

"A cruel twit of fate."

I laughed and it felt good, and the knot went away. Mostly. "Well," I mused, "maybe someone better will come along for both of us."

And right on cue, Bob came in and Susannah said, "Bob, I want you to meet my best friend."

I guess being in the papers must have gone to my head, or maybe I just wanted to inject some levity, but I said to him, "Hi, I'm Hubert, but of course you already know that."

And Susannah started laughing and I started laughing and Bob just stood there with a silly grin on his face.

Acknowledgments

Contrary to what those of us who write crime fiction might lead you to believe, murders are seldom solved by one person. Murder mysteries are also a team effort. The team for *The Pot Thief Who Studied Ptolemy* included Professor Ofélia Nikolova who knocked the rust off the Bulgarian I learned while living in Blagoevgrad and served as a human spell-checker for the Cyrillic portions of the story. Professor of Astronomy Martha Leake bought my first book, *The Pot Thief Who Studied Pythagoras*, and I rewarded her by making her work on the second. She reviewed my handling of celestial mechanics and telescopes. Carolyn and Lewis 'Andy' Anderson—she the local librarian in Questa, New Mexico, he an author and laid-off molybdenum miner—read the manuscript and provided both writing suggestions and proofing. Andy is also my gadfly, keeping my writing honest with all the subtlety of a cattle prod. Another gifted writer, Marie Romero Cash of Santa Fe, read the manuscript and gave me ideas and encouragement.

ACKNOWLEDGMENTS

Sally Kurrie of Valdosta was a trouper, proofing the manuscript while battling the flu. Finally, I relied as always on my daughter Claire and my wife Lai for their review of the story as it progressed and their proofing when it was finished. With such a great team, I can say—with no false modesty—that any errors that remain are mine alone.

About the Author

J. Michael Orenduff grew up in a house so close to the Rio Grande that he could Frisbee a tortilla into Mexico from his backyard. While studying for an MA at the University of New Mexico, he worked during the summer as a volunteer teacher at one of the nearby pueblos. After receiving a PhD from Tulane University, he became a professor. He went on to serve as president of New Mexico State University.

Orenduff took early retirement from higher education to write his award-winning Pot Thief murder mysteries, which combine archaeology and philosophy with humor and mystery. Among the author's many accolades are the Lefty Award for best humorous mystery, the Epic Award for best mystery or suspense ebook, and the New Mexico Book Award for best mystery or suspense fiction. His books have been described by the *Baltimore Sun* as "funny at a very high intellectual level" and "deliciously delightful," and by the *El Paso Times* as "the perfect fusion of murder, mayhem and margaritas."

THE POT THIEF MYSTERIES

FROM OPEN ROAD MEDIA

Available wherever ebooks are sold

O P E N R O A D

INTEGRATED MEDIA

Open Road Integrated Media is a digital publisher and multimedia content company. Open Road creates connections between authors and their audiences by marketing its ebooks through a new proprietary online platform, which uses premium video content and social media.

Videos, Archival Documents, and New Releases

Sign up for the Open Road Media newsletter and get news delivered straight to your inbox.

Sign up now at
www.openroadmedia.com/newsletters

CPSIA information can be obtained at www.ICGtesting.com
Printed in the USA
LVOW10s1532150415

434708LV00001B/122/P